THE MANY ADVENTURES OF MEILIN

THE MONKEY KING'S DAUGHTER

BOOK #1

T. A. DEBONIS

PUBLISHED BY:
Todd A. DeBonis • DVTVFilm
The Monkey King's Daughter®, is a registered trademark of Todd A. DeBonis

ISBN: 978-0-9678094-4-1 (0-9678094-4-4)

REGISTERED: US Library of Congress, WGA, USPTO

COVER ILLUSTRATION: John Forcucci, ©2009

WEBSITE: TheMonkeyKingsDaughter.com

ACKNOWLEDGMENTS: I'm extremely grateful to John Forcucci for his brilliant cover art, Monty Haas and Laurie Joy Haas for their diligent proofing, and all three for their overwhelming encouragement, support and longtime friendship.

PRINTED IN THE USA

For my two girls,
My-Linh and Anna

Preface

Once there was a monkey—but not an ordinary monkey, as monkeys go. Born from a stone that fell from the Heavens, this monkey soon became the ruler of all monkey-kind. But being the Monkey King was not enough for this arrogant scamp. He clamored for more. He quickly learned magic from mystic Taoist monks and ultimately, challenged the Heavenly Jade Emperor and the rest of the Chinese pantheon themselves. His monkey tricks and magic were so powerful that no one, not even the Heavenly Army, could defeat him. This made Monkey King even more arrogant—so much so, that he boldly challenged Buddha, himself. But Buddha easily defeated Monkey King and cast him down to earth where he remained buried under a tremendous mountain for over 500 years, until the day came that he might redeem himself by learning humility.

That day finally came and Buddha said he would allow Monkey to go free *if* he would escort and protect a young Monk carrying Sacred Scrolls from India to China, so that Enlightenment could be spread across all of Asia.

Monkey readily agreed, knowing that he would run away and take up his mischievous monkey ways again. However, Buddha could not be deceived and directed Guanyin, the Goddess of Mercy, to place a magical circlet around Monkey's head that would contract against his skull every time he made trouble for the young monk. The pain was unbearable, even for Monkey, and he ultimately learned along the long and arduous journey that there was more to life than just his own personal needs and desires.

In the end, Monkey's bravery and heroism allowed him to gain something far greater than magic and power—he gained true Enlightenment.

Now, all of Monkey's heroic adventures are well documented in the famous Chinese epic titled *"Journey to the West,"* by *Wu Cheng En* and you might ask yourself, why am I telling you this again?

I'm not.

This story isn't about Sun Wukong, the Monkey King—it's about his daughter, Meilin. Only, she doesn't know she's the Monkey King's daughter. In fact, she doesn't know she's half-monkey at all.

As far as Meilin knows, she's an ordinary high school freshman from Midland Hills, California, facing all the problems that bright young girls face at that age—insensitive teachers, flakey girlfriends, zits, too much homework, bad hair days, obnoxious boys...

But all of that's about to change.

You see, after the Monkey King gained Enlightenment, he fell in love with a young fairy maiden. Her name was Lijuan, a granddaughter of Guanyin. This angered many of the immortals in the Heavenly Palace who hadn't forgotten their first encounter with the Monkey King. But in particular, it angered the underworld demon god, Bull King. He and Monkey had tangled before and it nearly cost Bull King his life, as well as his domain. Bull King vowed that he would one day take revenge. How sweet it would be to kill the wife and daughter of his sworn enemy and topple the Jade Emperor at the same time!

With the Heavenly Palace about to be overrun by Bull King's massive demon forces, Monkey, in a desperate bid to save his wife and newborn child, combined his magic with Guanyin's and sent his family far into the future where they could be safe from harm. They were accompanied by one of Monkey's most trusted comrades, Zhu Bajie, affectionately known to most as Pigsy the Pig. Monkey remained behind to battle the demons that railed against him and threatened to tear the Heavenly Kingdom apart. And though it pained him to lose his family, he knew that they would be safe—or so he thought...

Chapter 1

Meilin Cheng burst into the kitchen with frantic urgency. "Mom!" she cried. "I can't go to school today! Just look at this!"

"Look at what, dear?" her mother said softly, not reacting to her 13-year-old daughter's plight. Lijuan was a classically beautiful Chinese woman with high cheekbones, brilliant black eyes and long black hair that she kept neatly bound with a red cloth hair-tie in a ponytail that reached all the way down to the small of her back. She was busy at the stove sautéing eggs, rice and bean sprouts for Meilin's breakfast.

"This!" Meilin wailed again, indicating a tiny bump on her forehead.

Meilin's mother shrugged. "I don't see anything."

"Are you kidding?" the slight teen cried. "It's the size of a mountain!"

"What's that?" her Uncle Zhu said, pausing mid-mouthful of his own heaping bowl of eggs, rice and bean sprouts that he had doused with half a bottle of soy sauce. Zhu Bajie was a fat and jolly man, whose moon-face, under a mop of unkempt thick bristle-like black hair, constantly beamed with a toothy smile.

"Uncle Z! Look at this!" Meilin insisted, bringing her face close to his.

"Ooo my, that's some big zit you got there. Want me to pop it?" he added with a snort.

"Eew, gross!" Meilin said, turning away from her uncle. "Mom?"

"Now, Meilin," her mother said calmly, "It's all part of growing up."

"Growing up? If this is part of growing up, then I don't want any part of it!"

"Ha!" said Zhu Bajie. "A zit's nothin'! I had tons of them when I was a little porker—I mean ahh, little kid. Just wait 'til your birthday comes and you start growin'..."

"ZHU!" Lijuan interrupted sharply. "Aren't you late for work?"

"Work?" Zhu said with a puzzled look on his face. "Oh, yeah. I almost forgot. There's a crate arriving at the shop today. Don't want to miss it."

Zhu Bajie stood up from the table and lumbered toward the sink while shoveling the remaining food in his bowl into his mouth with his chopsticks. He burped loudly before depositing his bowl atop the pile of other dishes waiting to be washed.

"Mmm... That was good." He paused and looked at Lijuan. "What's for lunch?"

"GO!" Lijuan said sternly, pointing the way from the kitchen.

"Oh, all right," Zhu Bajie grumbled as he waddled from the kitchen on his stubby legs. "I was just askin'."

Meilin shook her head at the sight. "Mom, don't you think Uncle Z might wanna cut back on the calories? It's not healthy."

"Oh, he's just portly," Lijuan replied.

"Mom, he's flat-out fat!"

"*I heard that!*" Zhu Bajie called from the other room. Meilin rolled her eyes and smiled, then refocused her attention on her own problem at hand.

"Seriously," Meilin restated. "Why does this have to happen to me now?"

"It's just a pimple, barely noticeable," Lijuan reassured. "Hurry up and eat or you'll miss the bus."

"Rrrr," Meilin growled. "Just what I need! And you know stupid Tiffany Edwards will use it to make fun of me."

Meilin's mother laughed. "And I suppose Tiffany's zit free?"

"Miss Perfect have a zit? *Pah-leeze!*" Meilin pouted.

Lijuan smiled and handed Meilin her breakfast bowl and a pair of chopsticks. "The things you worry about."

"She's awful, okay? Her and her dumb posse! They make it hard for everyone."

"Just ignore her."

"Easy for you to say," Meilin scowled. She deftly spun her chopsticks in her right hand and stabbed them into her food. Before lifting a mouthful to her lips, she paused. "Mom," she asked, "did you have a Tiffany when you grew up in China?"

Lijuan smiled and reflected a moment before answering. "I suppose. Ping was her name. She was always up to something rotten."

"Then you *do* understand," Meilin said.

"I understand that the bus will be here and you're going to miss it," Lijuan said. "So, chop-chop! Let's go! And stop worrying about what other people think..."

"It's what you think about yourself that counts," Meilin interrupted and finished for her mom.

Lijuan shook her head with a slight degree of weariness. She then wiped her hands on the light blue hand-towel that hung on the oven door and checked the hair-tie that bound her hair, making sure it was secure. Meilin always admired her mother's long silky hair and wore hers the same way, though not as long.

"Who knows, you might end up being friends someday," Lijuan added as she walked from the kitchen.

"Yeah, and pigs can fly," Meilin muttered to herself.

"Don't forget your joss sticks," her mother said as she disappeared around the corner.

Meilin took a deep breath, then silently sighed. Every day, a joss stick. Three to be exact. Sure they were Buddhists, but sometimes Meilin just couldn't see the point. This was California, not China. Sun, surf, *The Jonas Brothers, Miley Cyrus* and going to the Mall. Burning incense sticks and placing them on the small altar they had in their living room just didn't have any meaning for her— at least not like it seemed to have for her mother and Uncle Z.

And what was up with their obsession with that stupid statue of the Monkey King that sat alongside the miniature of Buddha? That was weird. It seemed as if they were praying to *it* instead. Meilin sometimes even thought she saw the hint of a tear in her mother's eyes when she looked at it. Even Uncle Zhu acted weird about it at times, always making sure it was clean and perfectly placed. The Monkey King was a silly legend anyway and quite frankly, Meilin was tired of hearing it, especially from Uncle Z. Everything was Monkey King *this* and Monkey King *that!* Uncle Z had so many Monkey King trinkets in his room that Meilin often wondered if he was trying to corner the market with hopes of one day making a killing on eBay. He was definitely a bit on the nutty side. Still, Meilin loved him, even if he was a kook.

Meilin loved her mother, too. And though Lijuan always put forth a smile, Meilin knew that there was an emptiness deep inside her mother that continually gnawed at her. Something in her mother's life was missing and Meilin just couldn't figure out what it was. Meilin used to think it was because of her, that being a single mom and raising a child was sometimes too much for her mother to bear—but that wasn't it. It was something deeper. Something had happened to her mother in the past and whatever it was, it must have been terrible. Yet when Meilin would broach the subject, her mother would divert the question and talk about something else. She wouldn't even talk about their family (if they had any) back in China. Outside of Uncle Z, as far as Meilin knew, she had no family at all. No Grandmother, Grandfather, father—no one.

And yes, what about her father? That was a subject that certainly never came up. Was he tall? Short? Good-looking? Ugly? Was he someone his mother loved who was killed in an accident—or did he just up and leave her? Meilin simply didn't know anything about her father and her mother certainly would never speak about him.

Uncle Z almost did, once. But just as quickly as he almost let something slip, he clammed up and started talking about something else. It really bothered Meilin not to know. When she was younger, she romanticized that her father was an undercover spy who disappeared on a secret mission and one day he'd reappear, rejoin the family and everything would be okay. But that was just a fantasy. As she grew older, she'd come to the conclusion that her father was probably a creep who left them. Good riddance if he was. She didn't need him anyway. Meilin just wished her mother could be happy.

Meilin finished her breakfast quickly. She then rinsed her bowl and set it on the rack. She wished she had time to wash all the dishes for her mother, but she didn't. The school bus was due to arrive at the corner in minutes. Meilin knew she had to hurry or it would leave without her.

As she rounded the hallway corner, Meilin grabbed her bulging two-toned jade green backpack, overstuffed with school books, notebooks, colored pencils and everything else she thought she might need and hefted it over her left shoulder.

She continued her path down the hall and turned into the living room. Her mother and Zhu Bajie were already there waiting. Zhu Bajie handed Meilin three smoldering yellow joss sticks. He then lit three for himself and three for Lijuan. Then each, in turn, raised the joss sticks to their foreheads three times, bowing slightly to the tiny Buddha statuette on the altar, silently whispering their prayers. They then placed the aromatic incense sticks into a small bowl filled with white sand where they would continue to smolder until consumed.

"Stop by the shop after school," Zhu Bajie said before Meilin could make her exit.

Meilin's face dropped slightly. "I got practice today."

Zhu Bajie smiled. "Oh?"

"Volleyball, remember?"

"Hmph," Zhu Bajie snorted. "Sure you wouldn't rather have me teach you Kung Fu instead? It's about time you learned. I know all the styles. Tiger, Snake, Monkey..." Zhu Bajie began dancing his massive frame around the room, striking several comical stances and making Bruce Lee-like noises. "But better than all those—is Pig-style!"

"Pig-style?" Meilin grinned. "No such thing."

"Is too!" Zhu Bajie grunted. "It's the most powerful style of them all. And luckily for you, I'm a Master!"

Zhu Bajie whirled in place striking another stance while uttering a tremendous *"Heeya!"*—his rear-end simultaneously taking out a corner table and a lamp with an equally thunderous crash.

"Oops!" Zhu Bajie said apologetically. "My bad."

Meilin looked at her mother, who shook her head at the mess on the floor.

"I can fix this," Zhu Bajie said, picking up one of the larger pieces of lamp and a table leg. "Pig-style just needs a little room, that's all."

"Yeah, you keep working on that," Meilin laughed. "I gotta go," she added, hurrying from the room.

"After school. Don't forget," Zhu Bajie called.

Meilin didn't answer. She didn't have to. She knew she'd be there. She couldn't refuse her uncle. She just hoped he wasn't going to show off another boring relic he managed to procure from some remote province in China—relics he never seemed willing to sell. And Meilin definitely hoped it wasn't going to be another stupid Monkey King fetish. The shop, like their home, was cluttered with them. In fact, Meilin couldn't understand how Uncle Zhu's business made any money at all. He hardly ever had customers and when he did, they never bought anything except some cheap Asian novelties—things like paper lanterns, chopsticks or bamboo backscratchers—all of which (if the customer bothered to look at the tiny sticker on the item carefully) were undoubtedly made in the Philippines! This is not to say that he didn't have anything worthwhile in his shop. He did. He was just loath to part with any of it.

The serious customers who came to the shop didn't come to see Zhu Bajie anyway. They came to see Lijuan. Lijuan was a skilled Chinese herbalist. And though the holistic tinctures and concoctions she prepared undoubtedly tasted as bad as they smelled, Lijuan had a reputation among the surrounding elderly Chinese community as someone who was no less than a miracle worker.

Still, for the very little money her customers paid for her services, Meilin was beginning to wonder how her mother's income sustained them, as well. It was another of the inconsistencies in their lives that she was slowly becoming aware of.

She wasn't mature enough to understand the household finances, but it was something that was creeping into her consciousness. They weren't rich by any stretch of the word. Yet, they weren't poor either. They had enough money for food, but never enough, it seemed, for the important things in life, like a PlayStation or widescreen TV, designer clothes or $200 *Uggs* shoes—all the things that many of Meilin's friends had and she didn't.

At least she had a computer, though getting that was a hard sell. If she didn't need it for school, she would have never gotten one. The only reason she had a cell phone was because it came with the business package the telephone company provided for the shop.

No, hers was a very traditional Chinese household—ancient Chinese. If only her mom would loosen up and "get with it", because, now that Meilin was in high school, it was really affecting her social standing amongst her peers. She was already pegged as a klutz and an academic nerd. But the clothes thing was really setting her back.

Lijuan and Zhu Bajie watched from the living room bay window as Meilin ran from the house for the bus that was pulling to a stop down the street. They saw another girl, Jessie Macintyre, Meilin's closest friend who lived two houses down, join her in the dash. She was slightly shorter than Meilin and had light brown hair.

"One more day," Lijuan said with trepidation.

"Then we'll know," Zhu Bajie said, coming to Lijuan's side. Yet, it wasn't a human form that stood next to her. It was the anthropomorphic form of a giant pig. Uncle Z was now his true self, Zhu Bajie, Pigsy the Pig.

"I'm frightened," Lijuan said. "What if..."

"Don't be," Zhu Bajie interrupted. "If it happens, it happens. If not, then so much the better for her."

Lijuan nodded, still keeping her eyes on her daughter who was now boarding the bus, laughing and talking with her friend. Zhu Bajie was right. If it happened, it happened. There was nothing she, or anyone, could do about it.

Chapter 2

With a short shriek, Meilin turned her back and covered her head in a failed effort to protect herself from the oncoming volleyball that Tiffany Edwards spiked at her. It was a futile move. The volleyball hit her hard, square in the back and rebounded across the court, out of play.

"Point! Red!" Coach Daniels cried after issuing a short blast from her coach's whistle. She was a young woman, 24 years old and new to the Athletic Staff at Midland Hills High School. Even so, she was already a favorite among the students who viewed the other gym coaches as prehistoric throwbacks.

The red-jersied team jumped with joy. The blue-jersied team, Meilin's team, groaned with their usual disappointment. Tiffany shot Meilin a smug look of superiority from her side of the net. She was tall, thin, beauty-pageant pretty, blond, popular and California tan—everything that Meilin wasn't, but wanted to be.

"In your face, Cheng," Tiffany said with a smirk.

Meilin grit her teeth. Her back stung and she wanted to cry, but she wouldn't give Tiffany the satisfaction.

"C'mon, Cheng!" Coach Daniels shouted at Meilin from side court. "We're not going to win any games if you keep turning away. Get tough! Face the ball head on!"

Meilin nodded as she recovered. Coach Daniels was right, of course. Meilin knew what she was supposed to do. It's just that she couldn't do it. In fact, she still couldn't figure why Coach Daniels didn't cut her from the team after the first scrimmage. She was absolutely horrible. Still, she liked the game—would like it more if she wasn't constantly targeted as the weakest link. Well, one of the weakest links, anyway. Jessie, wasn't much better. And in all reality, if Jessie wasn't on the team, she would have probably quit the first day. But Jessie liked to play and the two girls always tried to do everything together.

"Red serves, 19—7!" Coach Daniels called.

"C'mon, Meilin," Jessie whispered with encouragement. "We can do this. If I get the set, you go for the kill."

Meilin nodded with a half-smile at Jessie's effort to cheer her spirits. It was a good plan and for anyone else, it would have a chance. The only complication was that Meilin could barely jump high enough to touch the top of the net. Still, Meilin fantasized about blasting the volleyball right down Tiffany's throat. See how *she* liked it! Wouldn't *that* be something! But, Meilin knew, this was as likely to happen as pigs taking to the skies.

The ball was served long to the backcourt. It was received by red-headed Becky Williams, who bump-passed it up to the front.

"Set!" Jessie yelled as she set the ball up for Meilin right at the net. It was a perfect set, too. Meilin jumped up as high as she could to slap it over. But Tiffany read the move, and being 3-inches taller than Meilin, jumped at the same time to block—and spiked the ball down hard at Meilin just as it cleared the net on her side. This time, the ball hit Meilin on the side of her face and sent her down to the floor in a heap!

The hit rattled her and she saw stars. Meilin draped her arm across her forehead as she lay on her back, dazed.

"You jerk!" Jessie shouted, clenching her fists, ready to go after Tiffany in defense of her friend. But Coach Daniels was already on the court, blowing her whistle, taking control.

"Girls! Girls! We're all on the same team here!"

"You wouldn't know it the way Tiffany plays!" Jessie growled.

"It was a legal return," Tiffany shrugged. "It's not my fault she can't play!"

"That's enough!" Coach Daniels barked as she knelt by Meilin. "Red Team—locker room. Blue team—gather up the equipment, then go."

Tiffany shot Jessie a smug smile before turning and heading for the lockers, her posse surrounding her and laughing.

"You okay, Cheng?" Coach Daniels asked Meilin, who was still laying on the hardwood gymnasium floor.

Meilin nodded slowly as she struggled to sit up. "You did say, face the ball head on."

"I didn't mean it literally! You took a good shot to the head. Maybe the Nurse should have a look at you," Coach Daniels continued.

"It's nothing," Meilin insisted as she reached for Jessie's hand. Her friend latched on and hauled Meilin up to her feet. "I just missed, that's all."

Coach Daniels stood and examined Meilin's forehead and looked into her eyes, checking to see if they were dilated. "Well, okay... but if you have the slightest headache or feel unusual in any way, you get yourself looked at pronto. And I mean pronto! Sometimes head injuries don't manifest themselves until several hours later. Understand?"

Meilin nodded.

"All right then. Locker room."

Jessie guided Meilin toward the locker room by her elbow. "I hate that Tiffany," Jessie growled, after they were out of earshot. "I wish someone would pop her right in the nose."

"You mean her plastic nose?" Meilin grunted.

"Yeah," Jessie smiled. "She's always bragging how it cost her parents five grand."

"They should'a got her a personality instead." Meilin quipped.

Both girls giggled.

"Just once I'd like to see her get what she deserves," Jessie added.

"So would half the school," Meilin replied. "But I wouldn't hold my breath."

"Yeah. Some people are just born lucky," Jessie said. "Pretty. Rich. Gets everything she wants. Not that I'm complaining, it's just, I wish she wouldn't rub it in everyone's face."

"Yeah, well," Meilin replied, "it's like my Uncle Z says, '*She who tries to shine, dims her own light.*'"

"What's that supposed to mean?" Jessie said.

"Chinese for what goes around, comes around, I guess."

"Your uncle eats way too many fortune cookies," Jessie said.

"Tell me about it," Meilin agreed. "Next time, I'll set, you go for the spike," Meilin added as the two girls entered the locker room.

"Like there'll be a next time," a cold voice interrupted. It was Tiffany, accompanied by her wanna-be fan club, already dressed in their expensive designer jeans and blouses, making their grand exit.

"Coach Daniels already picked J-V first string," one of Tiffany's crew said.

"It's posted on her door," another confirmed.

"So?" Meilin said with a shrug.

"God, you're dense," Tiffany said dismissively. "Only six girls play."

"The six *best* girls," a third Tiffany wanna-be chimed.

"That be *moi* and company," Tiffany said with a smile, indicating her posse. "All the other dweebs—bench warmers," she added, referring to the rest of the girls in the locker room with disdain. "And then there's you."

"So?" was all Meilin could muster again.

"Yeah! So?" Jessie restated more strongly in her friend's defense. "What makes you think any of us won't get to play?"

"Because we want to win. The school wants to win. I want to win. And when the coach sees that I *can* win, she'll move me up to varsity and I'll get my letter, first year out. Then I can bail from this stupid sport and become cheerleader captain. Junior year—Prom Queen. Senior year—Prom and Homecoming Queen. See? I've got it all planned out. And no one, especially *Chopstick* here, is going to wreck it for me."

"School's more than just about you!" Meilin returned, angered by Tiffany's slur.

"No it's not. It's *all* about *me*," Tiffany stated smugly.

"Yeah, well it's a dim bulb that shines dim!" Jessie retorted, fumbling the thought.

Tiffany eyed Meilin and Jessie, shook her head with pity and pushed past. Her posse followed, laughing.

"Talk about dim bulbs," they heard one say as the clique disappeared around the corner.

"What *lose-ahs*," another said, with a Valley-girl drawl.

Meilin turned her head toward Jessie with a quizzical look. "Dim bulb shines dim?"

"Well—I needed a comeback," Jessie replied with a shrug. "I couldn't let her just walk away."

"Let me do the Asian stuff, okay?" Meilin said as they continued to their lockers.

"She's so full of herself!" Jessie said, fuming.

Meilin sat down heavily on the bench in front of her locker. "Yeah, well... She's right about one thing—I stink." Meilin pulled her loose-fitting blue jersey over her head, revealing the grey gym-shirt she wore underneath.

"Stink's such a harsh word," Jessie remarked musingly, also discarding her blue practice jersey. "You're more like *athletically challenged* or *god-awful* or..." Jessie began.

"I get the picture!" Meilin interrupted, holding up her hand to silence her friend.

Jessie shrugged. "Heck, we all stink. So what! It's fun, right?"

Jessie was right about that. Volleyball was fun, even if Meilin was horrible at it. But there was a practical reality Meilin had to face as well.

"Yeah. But school matches start next week and the team *will* want to win," Meilin stated. "If I quit now, at least they might have a chance."

"And give Tiffany the satisfaction? Heck no!" Jessie said. "You just need more practice!" Then Jessie added straight-faced, "Seriously—*a lot more practice!*"

Chapter 3

Atiny overhead bell jingled as Meilin pushed open the door to her uncle's shop. Meilin paused a moment before entering. Was she in the right place? Normally Zhu Bajie's *Heavenly River Imports* was an orderly disarray of vases, Chinese antique cabinets, armoires, small tables, trunks, hand-painted silk screens and assorted Asian curiosities—not to mention the shelves of Monkey King carvings, Buddha statues, lucky cats, Chinese piggybanks, calendars, and in the front, a table of cheap Asian kitsch. Now, the shop was in an even bigger state of confusion. Everything had been moved or pushed aside to accommodate a large plywood crate, standing at least eight feet tall and equally as wide, positioned at the rear of the shop.

"Uncle Z?" Meilin called cautiously.

Zhu Bajie popped his head around the side of the crate.

"Ahh, Meilin!" he said with excited glee. His huge frame waddled into view with a large screwdriver and hammer in hand. "Come on. You'll be the first to see."

Meilin smiled, caught up in her uncle's excitement. She dropped her backpack onto the floor and hurried to his side.

"What is it?" she asked.

"You'll see!" Zhu Bajie said. It was only then that Meilin saw that her uncle had already removed the bolts that held the front of the huge plywood crate in place.

Zhu Bajie used his screwdriver like a crowbar and with two quick pops, sprung the front panel free. He then slid it aside, stacking it against the side wall.

"Well?" Zhu Bajie said with expectation.

Meilin stood gaping at the sight. Finally she said, "Umm—what is it?"

"It's a door, of course!"

"A door," Meilin mouthed slowly with disbelief.

"A Gate actually," Zhu Bajie restated more correctly.

"Oh, a gate," Meilin repeated as if that correction changed its importance to her. "And you have it because?..."

"Because it's special. The only one of its kind."

"Oh, it's an antique," Meilin said, now looking at the wooden monstrosity as something more than another one of her uncle's imported oddities. Old Chinese gates were often displayed in upscale Asian antique shops and Meilin knew they sold for thousands of dollars to collectors or architects designing Asian-styled homes or garden courtyards. This one, however, was rather plain and not ornate in design. It was simple, made of weathered wood with rusted metal hinges. Meilin could tell that it was once lacquered in black and red, but the color had long since chipped and peeled away, probably due to exposure.

The only thing interesting about the gate was its lock. It wasn't traditional by any means, and quite enigmatic. There was no keyhole—just three small round holes spaced about one-inch apart along the top. Still, the piece was in such poor condition, no one in their right mind would buy it. Except her uncle. Well, perhaps he could restore it somehow.

"You think it will sell?" Meilin ventured, not wanting to hurt her uncle's feelings.

"Sell it?" Zhu Bajie snorted. "No-no-no. It's over three thousand years old. Besides, it's a gift."

"A gift?"

"Oh, there I go spoiling things," Zhu Bajie said, flapping his arms up and down like a duck. "It was supposed to be a surprise, but I couldn't wait to show you. It's for you. For your birthday!"

"You got me a giant old wooden gate for my birthday," Meilin said flatly. "Gee, that's ahh…"

"I know!" Zhu Bajie interrupted, his face beaming. "Isn't it great?"

Meilin could see that her uncle was genuinely proud of his gift—and that worried her. Perhaps he'd finally lost it. Moreover, it disappointed her.

"Is Mom here?" Meilin asked, her eyes still fixed on the travesty before her.

"Downstairs, with a client," Zhu Bajie said, still marveling his gate. He fished a rag out of his back pocket and set to work dusting it off.

Meilin spun on her heels and trotted to the short flight of stairs leading down to her mother's Chinese apothecary in the lower level of the shop.

There, she found Lijuan reaching into her hundred drawers of Chinese herbs, mushrooms, dried flowers, plants, roots, tree bark, seeds and other mysterious unnamable organics, skillfully selecting and weighing each before wrapping them in plain brown paper for an elderly Chinese woman who sat waiting patiently on the bench against the wall. The quarters were cramped and sometimes the line was long, but Lijuan gave each of her customers her undivided attention during both her diagnosis and the preparation of the cure.

Lijuan never asserted any medical claims to her art and was very cognizant of FDA and California State law. She was not a doctor and didn't pretend to be one. She was, however, Midland Hills' version of Chinatown's best kept secret. She was revered as a healer, and where, when, how and from whom her mother came by her skill was another of the many things that went unspoken in the household. Meilin knew that it was something that was not taught in school—even Chinese schools. So how did her mother come by the knowledge? Did she learn it from her own mother—again another nameless person to Meilin. Or did her mother learn it in a monastery, where perhaps she grew up as a child. Again, another mystery.

Meilin shook the thoughts from her head. She wasn't going to get caught up in that line of thinking right now. There was the matter of the gate.

"Mom," Meilin said softly, not wanting to interrupt her mother's train of thought, though still wanting her presence known.

Lijuan looked up, acknowledging her daughter, but didn't speak to her. Instead, she spoke in

Chinese to the old woman who waited patiently on the bench.

The old woman rose, approached Lijuan, and took the package of herbs.

Lijuan continued speaking softly in Chinese to the old woman, telling her how to prepare the infusion she wanted the woman to drink for a two week period, whereupon she should return to the shop for more.

The old woman bowed three times to Lijuan, then turned and retreated toward the steps. She paused momentarily in front of Meilin. Meilin could see that the woman had a kind face, though heavily wrinkled with her 90-years of age. Her eyes were moist with tears. The old woman smiled at Meilin, then gasped as if surprised with sudden recognition and whispered, "Wukong."

The old woman then quickly grabbed both of Meilin's hands tightly in hers as if doing so brought her comfort. She bowed once, then resumed her way up the stairs. "Wukong," Meilin heard her mutter again as she disappeared. "Wukong..."

Meilin eyed her mother with bewilderment.

Lijuan, took a deep breath and exhaled. There was sadness in her voice. "Cancer."

"Oh," Meilin said, feeling the sorrow of her mother's pronouncement. "Isn't there anything you can do?"

Lijuan shook her head. "No. The herbs I gave her will ease her pain, but she won't be back."

Meilin's heart sank. "Wow," she said. "And here I am coming down to talk to you about Uncle Z and his gate."

Lijuan shook her head with discomfort. "Ahh, the gate. Well, about that..."

"An iPod or something would have sufficed," Meilin interrupted with a touch of annoyance. "You know—something I could actually *use*. Why does he always do stuff like that? This isn't China and I'm not a Chinese kid. I'm an American."

"Chinese American," Lijuan corrected.

"You know what I mean, Mom," Meilin returned. Her eyes began to tear slightly. "And as far as the Chinese part goes, I don't know anything about it, anyway. I don't know where I was born, my grandmother's name, grandfather's name, my father—anything. You and Uncle Z never tell me anything. I'm sick and tired of not knowing where I come from. It's like we're in the Witness Protection program or something. It's not fair. I really hate it! I hate China and everything Chinese. I don't want to speak the language, study the Buddha stuff, any of it!"

"Meilin!" Lijuan said sternly. And that was all she needed to say. Meilin knew she had gone too far. She also knew that the subject matter was closed. Still, this wasn't the first time she'd expressed her feelings about her Chinese heritage. She could see her words hurt her mother deeply.

"Just once, I'd like to have a normal birthday." Meilin said softly, regaining her composure and wiping her eyes. "A friend over. Hamburgers instead of mooncake. See a movie. Go rollerblading. Be like the other kids. Is that too much to ask?"

Lijuan regarded her daughter for a long moment. "No, it's not." Lijuan finally said. "We owe you that much, at least. You can have a party and a friend over."

Meilin smiled and ran to her mother and hugged her close. "I'm sorry about what I said," she admitted. "I didn't really mean it like that."

"I know you didn't," Lijuan replied quietly.

"Hey-hey-hey!" Zhu Bajie interrupted from the top of the stairs. "Hugs all around and none for me?"

Meilin looked up at her uncle. "We're going to have a birthday party," Meilin announced.

"Oh?" Zhu Bajie replied, flashing a quick look at Lijuan. Lijuan nodded slightly. Zhu Bajie understood. His face broadened into a big smile. "Can we have hamburgers?"

Meilin's eyes welled up again, but this time with happiness. "Yes!"

"Good!" Zhu Bajie said, his smile stretching even wider. "I can eat a ton of hamburgers!"

Arm-in-arm, Meilin and her mother ascended the stairs. It was closing time.

"You know," Zhu Bajie remarked as they walked past the Gate, now fully exposed and unpacked from its shipping crate. "All this talk of hamburgers has made me hungry. Anyone else in the mood?" he added as he flicked off the shop's overhead lights and pulled the shop door shut behind him. "I'm thinking Peking Duck—or a meatball sub!" he continued, as they walked for the car parked in the rear of the building.

"Uncle Z..." Meilin giggled.

- - -

Inside the shop, everything was dark and still.

Suddenly, the Gate began to rattle—as if some unseen force behind it was trying to push its two doors open.

Then—silence. A long silence.

The gate doors rattled again.

The two doors strained apart ever so slightly from the invisible force within. Blinding blue and crimson light emanated from the opening and radiated into the shop.

The ancient rusted lock held firm, keeping whatever was behind the door from gaining access.

Then abruptly, the rattling ceased. The crimson and blue light disappeared and the door snapped firmly shut.

The shop was silent and still, once again.

Chapter 4

Meilin's digital alarm clock blared. 6AM. Meilin groaned as she hit the OFF button with a heavy arm. Groggy, with her eyes half-shut, she made her way to the bathroom.

She flicked on the light, then quickly flicked it off. It was far too bright and far too early for that.

She ran cold water in the sink, scooped a handful up and gave her face a good rub.

As the water dripped from her hands and chin, she forced her eyes open in order to look at herself in the mirror above the sink.

Then she screamed—a loud shrill scream that pierced the entire household.

Instantly, Lijuan was up from her bed and came running. Zhu Bajie, sleeping in the rear upstairs bedroom, came bounding down the staircase, propelled as if his near 300-pound body was shot out of a cannon. Both reached the bathroom simultaneously.

Inside the bathroom, Meilin held both her hands tightly over her face.

"What's wrong?" Lijuan cried as she rushed to her daughter.

"My face! My face!" Meilin wailed, still covering her face with her hands.

Lijuan struggled to pull Meilin's hands down so she could see.

"There's nothing wrong with your face," she insisted.

"But..." was all Meilin could manage between gasps. "In the mirror... I saw..."

"You saw what?" Lijuan asked. Her voice was calm and her tone was comforting.

Meilin opened her eyes and forced herself to look in the mirror again.

"But..." she said with utter bewilderment. Her face looked normal. "My face. I saw..."

Meilin went to the mirror and inspected her face closely with both hands. She then turned and looked at both Lijuan and Zhu Bajie. "It was—a monkey's face!" she said.

"A monkey?" Zhu Bajie repeated, with raised eyebrows.

"I'm not crazy!" Meilin insisted. "Maybe I was dreaming, but—I swear, it was so real…"

Meilin stared at both her mother and uncle, waiting for their reaction—their assurance that it must have been a dream. Instead they both stood mute, looking at each other.

"I'll put on the tea," Lijuan finally said.

"Better make it coffee," Zhu Bajie countered. "I've got a feeling we're all gonna need something stronger!"

- - -

At the kitchen table, Meilin screamed at the top of her lungs again. "I'm what!"

"Well, not a monkey per-se," Lijuan said delicately. "Sort of a half-monkey."

"In a very good way," Zhu Bajie added reassuringly.

"This is a joke, right?" Meilin smiled. "A birthday prank."

Lijuan and Zhu Bajie stared at Meilin and shook their heads, no.

"O-kay," Meilin said, playing along. "Now I know you're punking me."

Meilin scanned the kitchen. "You hid a camera, right? This is for one of those nutty reality shows." Meilin waved her hand and spoke to the imaginary audience, "Hello out there. My mom and uncle are mental. You can come get them. Take them to the funny farm."

"No camera," Lijuan said, matter-of-factly.

"Half-monkey," Zhu Bajie restated again. "At least that's the way it looks. We won't know for sure until you officially turn 14 later tonight."

"Oh... I see... Only half-monkey." Meilin stated calmly. "I guess that's okay, because if I was a full monkey, I wouldn't be sitting here," her voice escalated, *"I'd be in the zoo!"*

Zhu Bajie looked at Lijuan. "She's got a point," he shrugged.

Lijuan nodded in agreement.

Meilin pushed her chair back from the table and slowly stood. "I'm gonna go get ready for school now." And then she added. "I took Biology in eighth-grade. You can't cross a monkey with a human being. So, unless I'm part of some weird Chinese science experiment..."

Then Meilin paused, her mind racing. "OMG— that's it!" she realized. "That's why you left China and why you never talk about our family. I'm a science experiment!"

"Good grief, no!" Zhu Bajie said, shaking his large head.

"Gotcha!" Meilin said with vindication. "See? I can play this game, too. 'Cause the only way I could be half-monkey is if Dad was..."

"Meilin," Lijuan interrupted, tired of hedging with her daughter. "Your father is Sun Wukong—the Monkey King."

Deafening silence filled the room.

After a long moment, Meilin finally spoke. Her face and expression was sad and cold. "Mom, if you really didn't want me to have a birthday party, you could have just said no. I'd understand. You and Uncle Z didn't have to do all this to get out of it."

"Meilin, I..." Lijuan said, her eyes welling with tears.

"No," Zhu Bajie interrupted while standing. "There's only one way she'll believe."

Lijuan opened her mouth to protest, but Zhu Bajie raised his hand commandingly.

"Meilin, your father *is* Sun Wukong," Zhu Bajie said forcefully. "And I am his trusted companion, Zhu Bajie—Pigsy the Pig!" And with that, Zhu Bajie morphed into his true form.

Meilin didn't scream. She didn't run. She simply fainted and fell straight to the floor.

- - -

Meilin finally stirred and found herself laying atop her bed. Her digital clock glared 6:45 in big red numbers. Lijuan patted Meilin's head with a cold wet compress.

"Ooo, my head hurts. What happened?" Meilin said groggily.

"You fainted and hit your head," her mother replied.

Meilin reached up and felt her head with her hand. No bump. Just sore.

"I had the weirdest dream," she murmured.

"Hey, how's the patient?" Zhu Bajie said, coming into the bedroom. He was carrying a small wooden breakfast tray containing a cup of piping hot tea and two steamed rice cakes.

The sound of her uncle's voice made Meilin avert her eyes. But it wasn't the monster she had imagined who sat on her bed, but her jolly fat Uncle Z.

Feeling foolish, she nevertheless breathed a sigh of relief and reached for the tea.

"It was more like a nightmare," Meilin said, continuing her thought as she brought the hot tea to her lips. "I dreamed I was a monkey—and you..." she added, turning to her uncle, "you were a giant pig. Weird, huh?"

Meilin took a long draw of hot tea.

"Very weird," Zhu Bajie stated flatly. "But true! I am a pig!"

Meilin choked and sprayed hot tea across her bed.

"You mean, it wasn't a dream!" she coughed wildly.

"Afraid not," Zhu Bajie replied, as if his confirmation was nothing more than ordinary.

"O-M-G!" Meilin cried, as she sank back into her pillow.

"Maybe she should stay home from school today," Zhu Bajie said, turning to Lijuan.

Meilin's eyes snapped wide open. "OMG! School!" She sat up quickly, looking at the clock. 6:55AM. The bus would be coming in minutes.

Quickly, she hopped out of bed, grabbed her clothes and raced down the hall for the bathroom.

Her mother followed close at her heels. "Meilin, don't you think we should talk more about this?"

"No!" Meilin retorted. "This is a cruel joke and I'm not playing anymore!"

Meilin slammed the bathroom door shut and locked it. "I hate you!" she shouted through the closed door. "You've ruined my birthday! I hate you both!"

"Meilin!" Lijuan cried. She raised her hand to knock on the bathroom door, but Zhu Bajie stayed her.

"Leave her alone," he said. "It's gonna take a while for this to sink in."

Tears streamed down Lijuan's face as Zhu Bajie guided her toward the kitchen.

"My baby..." Lijuan sobbed.

"She didn't mean it," Zhu Bajie said, referring to Meilin's angry outburst. Then he added, "Besides, we knew this might happen."

Lijuan shook her head and wiped back her tears. Zhu Bajie was right. She'd prepared herself for the last fourteen years for this moment—both for the possibilities—and the ramifications. She even prayed to Buddha that it wouldn't happen, that her daughter would grow up normally, like any other girl. But she also knew who she was—and who Sun Wukong was. Even Buddha himself could not alter the fact of their union.

Lijuan also knew that Meilin was going to need both her and Zhu Bajie's help in order to come to grips with the reality of her situation. Meilin was the Monkey King's daughter. There was no escaping that fact now. But what would happen next was up to Meilin. There was a lot she needed to know and a lot she needed to learn. More importantly, there was a lot she needed to keep secret from the rest of the world—if she was to survive.

Chapter 5

"Well, I see someone's got the birthday blues," Jessie said, after sitting for five minutes on the bus next to her best friend in absolute silence.

Meilin exhaled heavily, turned her head away and stared out the window.

"Okay," Jessie said with a shrug. "If you don't wanna talk about it..."

"Something's going on at home," Meilin finally said, still gazing out the window.

"Oh?" Jessie replied, picking up on Meilin's distress. "Somebody sick?"

"No," Meilin said, looking down at her hands in her lap. "I told my mother that I hated her."

"Whoa! No way!" Jessie exclaimed in a hushed voice. "Why? Your mom's so cool!"

"It's complicated," Meilin replied.

"Well, I guess that beats what happened to me," Jessie said, holding up her right hand. Her middle and ring finger were bandaged together with medical tape.

"Eew," Meilin remarked with a wince.

"My dorky little brother slammed the fridge door on it."

Meilin winced again. "Broken?"

"Just bruised," Jessie replied. "You can imagine the words I uttered when it happened."

"Wow, I'm sorry I didn't notice it before," Meilin apologized.

"That's okay," Jessie said as the bus pulled into the entrance to Midland Hills High School. "You sure you don't wanna talk?"

Meilin shook her head, no, as she gathered up her heavy backpack.

"Okay then. See you third period," Jessie said standing. The two girls eased into the rush of students pushing for the exit at the front of the bus.

"Okay," Meilin replied, as two laughing boys cut between them in the exit line.

Once off the bus, Meilin made her way through the throng of arriving students, trotted up the stairs to the high school and headed inside for her locker. Her locker wasn't near Jessie's, due to the fact that unlike Middle School where everyone in her class was cordoned together, here, everyone was given lockers based on availability, as well as assigned homerooms. To Meilin's dismay, she and Jessie didn't share the same homeroom or academic schedule. The only classes they had in common were third period Gym on Wednesdays and Fridays, lunch, and fifth period Math.

Equally dismaying was the fact that Tiffany Edwards shared nearly all of Meilin's classes. To further the insult, Tiffany's locker was three doors down from hers.

Meilin spun her combination lock open and was busy unloading the books from her bag when she felt a prickle run up her spine. Tiffany!

"Look, it's *Chopstick*," Tiffany said, as she opened her own locker.

Meilin's face turned cold as she swung her locker door shut with a heavy hand. "Stop calling me that!"

"Ooo," the two girls in Tiffany's entourage echoed in unison.

"Better watch it, Tiff," the shorter Tiffany-clone advised. "She might Kung-Fu you."

"In that outfit?" Tiffany remarked. "*Pa-leez!*"

"Jerks," Meilin grunted, as she tried to push past the clique and head for her first class.

But the three girls blocked her path. When Meilin tried to go around them, they moved with her, still blocking her way. They crowded closer, backing Meilin against her locker. Meilin began to panic. What should she do? Moreover, what *could* she do? Nothing! She couldn't do anything but take it—and Tiffany knew it.

The bell rang.

Tiffany's grin tightened into a superior smile. The trio stepped back, allowing just enough space for Meilin to squeeze by.

"The Salvation Army phoned," Tiffany called as Meilin hurried down the hall. "They want their clothes back..."

Tiffany's entourage snickered and laughed, "Nice one, Tiff," and "Ya, good burn."

"Did you see her face? I thought she was gonna pee her pants..."

Meilin grit her teeth at the remarks and forced herself to keep walking. She wasn't going to give Tiffany the satisfaction of a reply—or let her see the tear in her eye. This was just another one of the games Tiffany played to intimidate Meilin. The other was her constant remarks demeaning Meilin's wardrobe.

Meilin's clothes were a sore point with her. Her mother always shopped for a bargain and that meant that Meilin was always dressed at least one or two years out of style. The only consolation, if one could call it a consolation, was that her mother no longer made Meilin wear the Chinese-style pants and blouses she wore in grade school. That style was okay for her mother—it suited her and reflected who she was. But Meilin wasn't her mother and she didn't want to be. Even as late as the sixth grade, Meilin was dressed like a waitress in a Chinese restaurant, which is when Tiffany started calling her *Chopstick*. It was just another thing she hated about her heritage.

Thinking of that started her thinking about what she said to her mother and uncle. Though there had been plenty of times she'd been upset with them in the past, usually about household rules or activities she was or wasn't allowed to participate in, she'd never uttered anything remotely as hurtful as what she said this morning. She loved her mother and her uncle. But the joke they pulled on her went too far. She just couldn't figure out how they did it—or why.

The whole thing was just too fantastic to believe anyway. Neither her uncle, and certainly not her mother, would ever do anything to hurt her. In fact, they were overprotective. If Meilin got so much as a scratch or bruise from falling off her bike, they were all over her with care.

So, what really *did* happen?

Certainly not what she thought happened. People can't turn into pigs and obviously, she didn't see a monkey in the bathroom mirror. If anyone was at fault, it had to be her. Maybe the emotional strain of turning fourteen had something to do with it? Or perhaps it was medical....

Yes—that had to be it! The hit she took to the head at volleyball practice. Coach Daniels said there might be a delayed reaction. She was hallucinating.

"What an idiot!" Meilin said out loud.

"Excuse me?" the boy she wove past in the hallway said.

"Not you—me!" Meilin replied as she kept on walking.

The boy, a junior, shook his head and resumed his path. "Ditz!" he grunted.

Of course! It was the only explanation. The entire incident was a hallucination brought on by yesterday's hit on the head. It obviously jumbled her brain.

Now Meilin was even more upset than before— but with herself. She owed her mother and uncle a big apology. She just hoped that after the way she acted and what she said, they would forgive her.

- - -

"Go-go-go!" Coach Daniels shouted as Tiffany Edwards and another girl strained to pull themselves up the 25-foot long climbing ropes suspended from the school's gymnasium ceiling. Tiffany was stronger than the girl on the rope next to her and touched the top of the supporting beam first.

"Nineteen seconds," Coach Daniels announced.

Tiffany and the other girl slid down their ropes.

"Very good," Coach Daniels added when the two girls touched down on the floor mat. Tiffany took the praise without reaction, as if it was expected.

Tiffany and the other girl returned to the rear of the two lines of waiting girls.

Meilin and Jessie were up next. Rope-climbing wasn't the activity Meilin was hoping for in Gym today. She'd rather run track outside, but Miss Daniels had other ideas. It was "Physical Fitness Friday" and everyone was being graded on their performance—as if it really mattered since 90% of the girls couldn't climb more than half-way up anyway.

"Okay," Coach Daniels said as Meilin and Jessie approached. "Nineteen seconds is the time to beat. Whoa!" she paused, noticing Jessie's taped fingers. "What happened to you?"

"Nothing," Jessie replied.

"You sure you can do this?"

"Piece of cake," Jessie stated confidently.

"How about you, Cheng? How's the head?"

"Fine, Coach," Meilin lied.

"Okay. Nineteen seconds is the record. Let's see if either of you can give me sixteen. On your mark..." Coach Daniels readied her stopwatch.

Jessie and Meilin grasped their ropes.

"Last one to the top," Jessie challenged with a wink. Meilin smiled. Of all the girls who stood a chance at beating Tiffany's time, it would be Jessie. She was strong, she was fast and she was light. She just wasn't tall—which was one of the reasons she played volleyball so poorly. Still, her size never stifled her enthusiasm.

"Go!" Coach Daniels commanded.

Instantly, Jessie was on her way. Within the first seconds, she'd already outdistanced Meilin.

Below, it was obvious to the class that Jessie might indeed beat Tiffany's time. They cheered Jessie on, much to Tiffany's annoyance.

Coach Daniels was equally impressed with Jessie's ability and shouted out the time, "12—13—14..."

Meilin, herself, was spurred on by Jessie's aggressiveness and put extra effort into her own attempt. She knew she couldn't catch Jessie, but had closed the distance between them to one body length.

"15—16—Come on Jessie!" Coach Daniels shouted.

Jessie reached the top of her rope. She did it! With victory in her grasp, Jessie quickly reached out with her good hand to slap the support—and missed! The force of her swing caused her weakened taped hand to lose its grip and she fell.

Everyone below gasped in horror as Jessie plummeted straight down.

They gasped again when, by some miracle, Meilin deftly latched onto one of Jessie's flailing arms and plucked her midair from certain serious injury.

It all happened in a flash. But to Meilin, it was as if time itself stopped. She saw her friend miss and fall. She saw the surprise and horror on Jessie's face as the ground raced up towards her. Meilin also saw herself move instinctively and effortlessly like an acrobat, as if she had all the time, ability and strength in the world to reach out and easily pluck her friend to safety.

Jessie dangled twenty feet above ground in Meilin's iron grip. Jessie's expression was initially one of utter amazement and relief. But her eyes quickly widened at what she saw. Was it simply shock or were Meilin's right forearm and hand covered in—fur?

Meilin saw it, too. Quickly she swung Jessie close enough to the rope so that her friend could latch on. Jessie then slid down, Meilin, following close after.

Jessie collapsed on the mat breathing hard. Coach Daniels and the class quickly gathered around to see if she was okay, which gave Meilin the opportunity she needed to slip away and run to the girls' locker room.

Meilin ran into the locker room covering her right forearm and hand with her shirttail. She ran into one of the empty bathroom stalls near the showers, slammed the door shut and locked it.

Breathing hard, she hazarded a look at her hand and forearm. *They were covered in fur!* Short, thick, brown and golden monkey fur! It was on the inside of her hand too. Even her nails were slightly pointed and sharp.

"Oh my God!" she gasped. Meilin started to hyperventilate as she stared at her arm and hand. "What's happening to me?" she cried.

"Meilin!" Jessie shouted as she entered the locker room, looking for her friend.

Meilin didn't answer.

"Meilin!" Jessie called again. "Coach wants to know if you're okay?"

Jessie quickly scanned the locker aisles for her friend. Finally, she spotted Meilin's feet at the base of the bathroom stall.

"Hey!" Jessie said, slapping her hand on the stall door.

"Go away!" Meilin cried from inside.

"Like heck!" Jessie replied. "Open up!"

"No!"

"Open up or I'll climb right over the top!" Jessie declared.

Still, Meilin didn't make a move.

"Okay..." Jessie said.

Before Jessie could reach up for the top of the door, she heard the latch slide open.

Tentatively, Jessie pushed the stall door open and found Meilin sitting atop the toilet, tears streaming down her face, still trying to cover her arm.

"Don't look," Meilin begged.

But Jessie did look; she couldn't help it.

"My God! What's happened to you?"

"I don't know," Meilin said. "Something... I just don't know what!"

"Jeez!" Jessie whispered, getting a closer look at Meilin's arm and hand. "I thought I imagined it—but it's real!"

Meilin pulled her hand and arm closer to her body.

"Please go..." Meilin begged.

"No way!" Jessie said firmly. "You saved my life up there. Besides, we're BFFs, right? You think a little hair on your arm would change that? What can I do to help?"

"Help me get out of here. I need to get to the shop."

"You can't leave school. You won't make it past Security without a pass. Unless..."

Jessie grabbed Meilin's good arm and pulled her to her feet. "Come on," she said confidently. "I got a plan."

Meilin followed Jessie out of the locker room, concealing her right arm completely inside her shirt.

With Jessie in the lead, the two skirted silently down the hallways toward a side exit to the school. When they reached the intersection of the East hall, Jessie held up her arm, signaling stop.

Jessie then peered carefully around the corner. At the end of the corridor was one of the school's hired security guards sitting with his feet up on the small desk near the glass exit doors that led to the side parking lot. Quickly, Jessie withdrew and turned to Meilin.

"There's only one," she whispered.

Meilin nodded.

"You're gonna tell me what's going on later, right?" Jessie said expectantly.

"If I can," Meilin replied. "Right now, I don't know myself."

Jessie nodded, then motioned Meilin to stay put, but be ready.

Then, with a wink, Jessie was in motion. She rounded the corner shouting urgently, "Hurry! I think there's a fight in the boys' room!"

In an instant, the Rent-a-Cop was on his feet. He ran toward Jessie, who took off running toward a distant restroom located in the opposite direction.

"This one down here!" Meilin heard Jessie say as her voice trailed away.

Focused on following Jessie, the guard raced past Meilin without noticing her.

Meilin then slipped around the corner, ran down the hall and pushed through the double-glass doors.

What both girls failed to note was that the doors were also monitored by security cameras.

Chapter 6

"**U**ncle Z!" Meilin exclaimed as she burst through the front door of Zhu Bajie's *Heavenly River Imports.*

Zhu Bajie had the shop's cordless phone to his ear. "Ah, yes, she just walked in. Yes, thank you," he finished, ringing off. "That was the school," he said to Meilin. "Seems you're missing."

"Ya think?" Meilin snapped, holding up her fur-covered forearm.

"Ah..." Zhu Bajie said, comprehending the situation.

""What's going on!" Meilin demanded. "And where's Mom?—Mom!" she yelled and started for the stairs leading down to her mother's apothecary.

"She's not here," "Zhu Bajie stated. "She's out buying you a present."

Zhu Bajie's revelation altered Meilin's footsteps. She changed direction, crossed the floor and stopped a few paces in front of him, standing near the Gate. She waited for an explanation.

"Are you in any pain?" Zhu Bajie asked.

"No," Meilin answered, still breathing hard. She wasn't. She felt physically fine. In fact, she felt more than fine. She felt—powerful. It wasn't a conscious feeling, but just something that was there, a strange energy coursing through her body.

"Good," Zhu Bajie said calmly. "Does anyone else know?"

"Only Jessie," Meilin replied.

Zhu Bajie exhaled heavily at the revelation.

"She won't tell anyone," Meilin insisted, noting her uncle's concern. "I know she won't."

Meilin then explained what happen in gym class, how Jessie fell, how she saved her—as if doing so was second nature, and how Jessie helped her slip away.

"Okay," Zhu Bajie nodded. "I'll trust her. For now."

Meilin regarded her uncle for a long moment. "Uncle Z," she finally said, looking straight at him. "I need to know the truth."

"Yes," Zhu Bajie said, wrapping a large arm around her shoulders and gently drawing her close. "Yes, you do!"

Zhu Bajie guided Meilin over to a small blue and green, dragon-embroidered Chinese-style love seat he had for sale a few feet away.

After motioning Meilin to sit, Zhu Bajie went to the front door, flipped the OPEN sign to CLOSED and locked it. He then returned and sat on the other end of the love seat and faced Meilin.

"Before I begin," Zhu Bajie said, "you need to know that your mother loves you more than anything in the world..."

"This," Meilin said, indicating her furred arm, "is how she loves me?"

"Meilin," Zhu Bajie said in a sincere yet forceful voice. "Your mother risked her life for you. She placed herself in death's way to keep you from being killed. She sacrificed everything for you— her home, her life, her husband. And she'll do it again, should the need ever arise."

"Mom?" Meilin said with concerned astonishment.

"Oh yes," Zhu Bajie repeated with absolute sincerity. "Your mother gave up everything for you."

"But..." Meilin mouthed.

"Shh," Zhu Bajie interrupted. "I'll get to all that in a minute. First, we're gonna take care of that arm. Remember those Chi-centering exercises I've tried to teach you since you were little?"

Meilin nodded. "The ones I thought were silly and laughed at?"

"Yup," Zhu Bajie said, remembering the fuss Meilin always made. "Let's do one now. Hold up your arm..."

Meilin complied and held her arm bent, chest high, out in front of her.

"Now concentrate. Focus your mind and balance your thoughts. See your arm as you want to see it—as you want it to be."

Meilin focused herself and stared at her arm. It was hard to clear her mind, but somehow, with her uncle calmly encouraging her to breathe deeply and evenly, to let all her thoughts go to her center and find her Tao—she managed to do it. The fur on her forearm and hand receded and disappeared as if it was never there. Even her fingernails returned to normal.

Meilin's face beamed with awe—and relief.

Zhu Bajie smiled. "See? It's easy."

"But how can this be real? I mean, come on... The Monkey King? It's a story."

"Is it?" Zhu Bajie said. "You're the one sitting here with monkey fur on your arm. Just be thankful you didn't sprout your tail," he added casually.

"A tail!" Meilin burst out. "Oh my God..."

"Your dad has a tail," Zhu Bajie said with a grin. "A long fuzzy one. There's no reason to think that you won't sprout one, too. Like father, like daughter, they say."

"Oh—my—God," Meilin repeated again.

Then Zhu Bajie became serious. "Look, just because the Monkey King's a legend doesn't mean that it's not true. It all happened pretty much as written—except for what happened next. And I should know, because I was there."

Zhu Bajie then summarized for Meilin the events that followed their adventure to bring the Sacred Scriptures to China that culminated with Sun Wukong attaining Buddhahood.

"All was at peace in the Heavenly Kingdom and the Court of the Jade Emperor. Your father went on to pursue tranquility within the Tao and divided his time between his monkey kingdom and the Heavenly Court.

"I, on the other hand, devoted myself to what I did best—eating and pursuing, well, let's just say some of my old ways. I never achieved the level of Enlightenment your father did.

"It was on one of his visits to the Palace that your father first ran into your mother. I guess it was love at first sight."

"With a monkey?" Meilin interjected.

"With the Monkey King," Zhu Bajie corrected. "Remember, your father is Master of the 72 Transformations. He can be anything he wants to be—plant, animal, man, woman, rock, flame..."

"Okay-okay. I get the picture," Meilin interrupted again. "He can look like Prince Charming if he wants. What about Mom? Didn't she know he was a monkey?"

"He's not a *monkey*, as you so simply put it. He's the Monkey King. An immortal. I mean, sure he's a monkey, but—*ah*—you know what I mean."

"And Mom? Is she a monkey, too?" Meilin asked.

"No. She's born of the Chinese fairy-folk. But more than that, she's the granddaughter of Guanyin, the Goddess of Mercy."

"Whoa!" Meilin exclaimed. She at least knew that name from Chinese lore.

"Whoa, is right!" Zhu Bajie agreed. "Your grandmother's a pretty heavy hitter up there."

"Then..." Meilin said, trying to absorb what Zhu Bajie was telling her. "Why all this?" she asked, indicating her surroundings. "Why are we here?

Why aren't we up there—back there—or wherever we're supposed to be?"

"Because a really nasty demon, named Bull King, wants you, your mother and your father dead. Not to mention anyone else who might stand in his way and prevent him from taking over the Heavenly Kingdom—if he hasn't already."

"You mean you don't know!" Meilin cried, rising from the love seat with sudden concern. Now that she'd learned that she had a family, a real father as well as a real grandmother—had she suddenly lost them as well?

"No..." Zhu Bajie painfully admitted as he also rose. "I don't."

Zhu Bajie walked slowly over to the ancient Chinese gate that stood nearby.

"You were just born when Bull King's demon army assaulted the Jade Emperor's palace," Zhu Bajie began. "Sha Wujing—that's your other uncle—and I were visiting your mother in her hillside home when a raiding party attacked.

"We fought them off, helped your mother gather you up and began heading for the Palace. But Bull King's forces intercepted us again and with only two of us to defend against sixty, we were outnumbered and soon beaten. When Sha Wujing and I both went down, your mother shielded you with her own body just as a demon captain was about to cut you in two. I was horrified. There was nothing I could do to save you or your mother. Then, miraculously, your father appeared just as the blade was about to strike true. He single-handedly obliterated the entire squad with such fury that I'd never seen in him before. No one would ever harm you or Lijuan when he was around.

"We then flew into the courtyard of the Jade Emperor. But it wasn't safe there either. The palace was under full assault and about to fall. Your father was needed at The Jade Emperor's side, yet he was torn between his duty and his family. That's when your grandmother appeared and offered a drastic solution. She created a gate—*this* Gate," Zhu Bajie said, pointing to the ancient relic before him.

"Combining her magic with your father's, she offered a way to protect you and your mother from certain death should the Kingdom fall that day by sending you into the future where you could never be found. It also meant that your mother and father would never see each other again. It was their love for you that allowed them to easily make that sacrifice. You would be protected at all costs. To make doubly sure, your father sent me along, as well."

Tears streamed down Meilin's face as Zhu Bajie concluded his story. Zhu Bajie motioned her to come to him. She ran over and buried her face into his massive chest.

"So you see," Zhu Bajie said softly. "Your mother—and your father, have given everything for you."

Meilin continued to cry. "How could I have said that I hated her?"

Zhu Bajie tilted Meilin's face up with a fat thumb. "She knows you didn't mean it," he said, wiping her tears away with his hand. "Besides, with all of this hitting you at once, we kind of expected it anyway." Then he added in a happier tone, "Dry your tears. It's your birthday. And we want to be happy when your mother gets here, right?"

Meilin forced a smile and nodded. She then looked at the Gate. It had new meaning for her now. Before it was just a piece of junk, another waste of money in her uncle's collection. But now, it represented a link to her family. It was a piece of the puzzle that had daunted her mind since early childhood—who she was, and where she came from. Meilin also found herself loathing the Gate. For though it had saved her, it also cut her off from the family she would never know.

"Uncle Z," she said. "If we came through this Gate, can't we go back? I mean, does it still work?"

Zhu Bajie shook his head. "No. It was a one-way trip—which reminds me..." Zhu Bajie said, crossing quickly to a wall shelf near the rear of the Gate. He lifted a narrow black velvet box from the shelf and presented it to Meilin. "I saved this for you for 14 years—well, a couple thousand if you do the time-shift math stuff, but—happy birthday."

"What is it?" Meilin said as she took the velvet box and carefully opened it.

Zhu Bajie didn't answer.

"Oh..." she gasped. Inside the box were three jade hair sticks. Two of the hair sticks were about six inches in length and topped with intricately carved cylindrical Tibetan-style prayer wheels. The third was longer and slightly thicker, the length of a chopstick, and was capped in gold.

"These belonged to your grandmother," Zhu Bajie said. "They're also the keys to the Gate. She gave them to me just before I stepped through," Zhu Bajie finished with a heavy voice. "I'm certain she would have wanted you to have them."

"They're beautiful," Meilin said, carefully lifting the jade hair sticks from their case. She gingerly held them in her hands as she examined them.

The jade felt warm to her touch. Then, almost unconsciously, Meilin walked over to the Gate and inserted each of the jade hair sticks into the keyholes on top of the lock. She placed the larger one in the center. The old rusted lock clicked inside and released.

Meilin stepped back, as if she expected something magical to happen.

Nothing did.

Her heart sank. Zhu Bajie was right. It was a one-way trip. Whatever magic her grandmother and father may have worked thousands of years ago, was gone. It was one more affirmation that the family she just discovered was lost to her forever.

Zhu Bajie stepped forward and took Meilin's hand. He turned and guided her away from the Gate for the stairs that led to her mother's apothecary below.

"Come on," he said. "Your mother wants you to have a party. Help me bring up a table and some chairs from the storage closet. And there's soda in the fridge. We'll get everything set up before she gets here and surprise her."

Meilin's spirits brightened. Yes, that was a good idea. Then, during the happiness of the party, she'd make up for what she said and everything she thought.

While Meilin and Zhu Bajie worked in the downstairs storage closet, moving boxes and overstock in order to get at the long fold-out table and folding chairs buried in the back, something upstairs started to happen.

The Gate began to rattle. A surge of blue energy, much like lightning, arced across the door. The doors vibrated and the crimson and blue light that appeared the night before, began to emanate from the center seam where the two doors met.

At the same time, Lijuan, negotiating two large brown paper bags filled with food and presents, struggled to turn her key in the shop's front door lock. The lock clicked and she pushed the door open with her rear and walked backwards into the store.

"Zhu? Meilin?" she called out.

Downstairs, Meilin and Zhu Bajie heard her call. Meilin smiled broadly. "Be right up, Mom!" she responded.

Meilin and Zhu Bajie yanked the table they were wrestling with free from the boxes piled against it when they heard a terrible explosion.

"ZHU!" they heard Lijuan cry. There was unspeakable terror in her voice.

Instantly Zhu Bajie bolted from the closet and raced for the stairs. Meilin was close on his heels.

When they got to the top of the stairs, absolute horror filled Meilin's eyes. The Gate was wide open, and three dark goblin-faced demons, dressed in ancient Chinese battle-armor, were wrestling with a struggling Lijuan.

"Mom!" Meilin screamed.

Zhu Bajie moved fast. Instantly, he morphed into his true Pig form. His trusty weapon, Jiu Chi Ding Pa, his nine-toothed rake of pure ice-metal, materialized in his hands. He launched himself at the demons holding Lijuan. But he wasn't quick enough. The lead demon easily repelled Zhu Bajie by throwing a small spherical energy grenade. The energy ball hit Zhu Bajie square in the chest and propelled him backward twenty feet to the floor. It was all the time the demons needed to retreat through the swirling portal.

It was then that the lead demon saw Meilin. But there was not enough time to risk grabbing her. Zhu Bajie was already on his feet and charging forward. Half-a-prize was better than no prize at all. The demon stepped backward into the swirling vortex and vanished.

"Mom!" Meilin screamed as she ran forward. "I thought you said the Gate didn't work!" she railed at Zhu Bajie.

"It's not supposed to!" Zhu Bajie roared.

"What can we do!" Meilin demanded.

"You're doing it now! Look!" Zhu Bajie said, pointing at Meilin.

Meilin paused and looked at her arms. They were becoming completely covered in fur. Her hands were changing, too. So was her face.

"I'm going Monkey!" Meilin exclaimed with more anger in her voice than astonishment.

"That's my girl!" Zhu Bajie replied. "Hold that thought, 'cause where we're going, you're gonna need it!"

"We're going in there?" Meilin cried with trepidation.

"It's the only way to save your mother!" Zhu Bajie replied. "Hurry! Before the portal closes! And grab those keys!"

Zhu Bajie stepped halfway into the vortex and held out his hand, waiting for Meilin. She didn't need to be told twice. Her mother was in danger. Meilin took a deep breath and grabbed the three jade hair sticks. She then latched onto Zhu Bajie's meaty pig hand and stepped through the portal with him.

At the same time, Jessie pushed through the shop door carrying Meilin's backpack.

"Hey, Meilin," she said, "You left your books at...school...to...day..." She paused mid-sentence as she witnessed Meilin stepping through the swirling portal. The two girls exchanged a brief glance—Jessie's, one of stunned disbelief—Meilin's, one that seemed to say—goodbye.

As soon as Meilin stepped completely through the portal, it vanished and the Gate doors snapped shut.

Jessie dropped Meilin's backpack on the shop floor and slowly backed out the door.

Chapter 7

The trip through the void was fairly instantaneous. Meilin felt the pressure of a tremendous static discharge ripple through her body. It wasn't painful. It seemed to liquefy her corporeal form to the point where it could be pulled or stretched from one reality into the next, like a raw egg being blown out of its shell through a small hole.

Then, just as quickly, the viscous sensation ended. Meilin found herself standing on the other side of the Gate in a rundown stone-walled courtyard garden inside the Heavenly Palace, still holding her uncle's hand. It was pitch dark, the dead of night. The only illumination came from nearby torches burning in the garden.

"Down!" Zhu Bajie ordered, as he pulled his hand free and reset his grip on his rake. Meilin did as he commanded and crouched low, allowing Zhu Bajie a better chance to shield her with his body.

Two dog-faced demons guarding the Gate attacked. Zhu Bajie whirled his nine-toothed rake like a helicopter rotor, knocking both of the demon guards on their heads, dazing them. He then body-slammed each with his enormous belly and sent them flying into a nearby koi pond.

"Now *that's* Pig-style!" he said with satisfaction.

But more guards heard the commotion and could be heard running their way.

"Rats!" Zhu Bajie cursed. "Looks like the Palace fell after all! We gotta get outta here!"

With that, he conjured a small cloud at his feet.

"Hop on!" he commanded and pulled Meilin onto the small cloud without waiting for her to comply. Instantly the cloud launched itself high into the sky, speeding up and out of the Palace garden courtyard toward the safety of the nearby mountains.

"O-M-G!" Meilin cried with amazement, holding Zhu Bajie's arm tightly with both hands so she wouldn't slip and fall from the cloud that whizzed through the night sky. "Pigs *do* fly*!*"

"You bet we do!" Zhu Bajie laughed. "And so can you. You just have to learn how."

"Where are we going?" Meilin asked.

"I don't know," Zhu Bajie replied, keeping a watchful eye for any demon that might have enough magic to pursue them. None were. "Best thing we can do is hide out for a while and see what's going on."

"But what about Mom?" Meilin demanded.

"Bull King won't hurt her!" Zhu Bajie said firmly. He left the "*not yet*" part out of his remark.

"How can you be so sure!" Meilin cried. Zhu Bajie could see the extreme concern in Meilin's eyes.

"Because he needs her," Zhu Bajie replied. "He had no reason to take her from the future unless he needs her here in the past. Once we know why, we'll have a better chance at rescuing her."

Zhu Bajie set his flying cloud down into the safety of a dense forest of tall bamboo on the far side of the jagged mountain range, several miles from the Heavenly Palace.

"They won't track us here," he said confidently. "Do you still have those keys?"

Meilin nodded, discovering that she still gripped them tightly in her left hand—her left monkey hand.

"Better put them in a safe place," Zhu Bajie advised.

Meilin did as told, winding her long black hair into a ponytail. She then gathered it up on the back of her head and secured it with the jade hair sticks, as she had often seen her mother do.

Meilin's attention then returned to her physical appearance. "I'm all monkey'd-up" she grumbled, looking at her furred arms and touching her face.

"You look fine," Zhu Bajie reassured. Then he added with a smile, "For a monkey..."

"Uncle Z!" Meilin complained.

Zhu Bajie snorted a pig-laugh. "And, your tail's showing!"

"Ahh!" Meilin squeaked, looking over her shoulder at her backside. Sure enough, she had a tail. "O-M-G!" was all she could say.

"Let's get moving," Zhu Bajie said. "We shouldn't stay in one place too long."

Zhu Bajie took the lead. Meilin fell in step behind.

"Where do we go?" she asked.

"I don't know," Zhu Bajie replied. "But clobbering those guards made me hungry. Let's look for something to eat."

Her uncle had a point. Meilin missed lunch period in school and didn't have dinner. She was hungry.

Meilin quickly admonished herself for thinking of her own needs, especially since her mother was being held captive—who knows where! She silently prayed that she was all right and that

Zhu Bajie could figure a way to save her. And if he did, how would they get back home? This was a crazy place, not like the world she grew up in. She wanted to go home—*her home*—California! But she knew she couldn't. Not until she found her mother.

"It's all my fault!" Meilin said heavily. "If I didn't put those hair sticks into the lock..." She glanced up at her uncle, "None of this would've happened!"

"No!" Zhu Bajie returned. "I gave you the keys. If it's anyone's fault, it's mine! Still, I don't understand it. The Gate was inactive. It would take someone with far more magic than Bull King to bring it to life. The only problem is—who?"

Zhu Bajie's pig ears broadened their angle slightly. There was a noise—a very faint noise from above.

"Walk close to me," Zhu Bajie whispered in a hushed commanding tone.

Meilin's eyes widened. Her monkey ears picked up on it, too. Above them, high in the bamboo canopy, something was moving. Meilin stepped closer to her uncle. She let her eyes glance upward, searching the bamboo tops against the night sky.

And then she saw them—dark shadows silently and effortlessly leaping from bamboo to bamboo in the canopy above. The shadowy shapes were following their every step, altering direction as they did.

There were at least twenty, Meilin estimated, and their numbers were increasing with every step she and Zhu Bajie took.

Zhu Bajie could count too, and he didn't like the mounting odds.

"Run!" he shouted. Meilin didn't need to be told twice. She broke into a full run alongside her uncle. For as fat as he was, Zhu Bajie was fast. The two zigzagged their way through the dense bamboo in an effort to outdistance whoever was tracking them from above. Meilin almost tripped and fell several times as she ran. But, no matter which direction they went, they could not shake the leaping shadows that dogged them.

Suddenly, the ground around them erupted. Walls of cut bamboo shafts shot up from the forest floor like knives, completely encircling them. It was a trap and Meilin and Zhu Bajie had run right into it!

The dark shadows from above swiftly descended and ringed the inside perimeter of the bamboo walls. There were at least thirty of them.

A heavy rope net then fell from the bamboo canopy, pinning Meilin and Zhu Bajie to the forest floor.

Zhu Bajie struggled to stand under its weight and cast it off.

The dark shadows advanced, swords drawn and ready. As they stepped closer Meilin could see—they were *monkeys*!

"Prepare to meet your doom!" Zhu Bajie shouted defiantly, as he continued with little success to lift the heavy rope net up and cast it aside.

"*Meet your doom?*" a cold voice responded. A tall figure materialized out of the shadows twenty feet before them. The ninja-like monkeys parted rank around him as he approached. "After all these years, that's the best you can do? *Meet your doom?*"

Zhu Bajie recognized the voice and stopped struggling. He exhaled heavily. "Hello, Sandy..."

"Hello, Pigsy," Sandy replied, stepping close enough for Meilin to see his face. Sandy looked very much like a human in physical stature, tall, thin, and his face, though somewhat kind, had demon-like features as well. He was dressed in a dark blue monk's robe.

"Stuck?" Sandy asked.

"Of course not!" Zhu Bajie grunted. "All part of my strategy to draw your men closer before I made my move."

"Oh," Sandy nodded. "And how's that working for you so far?"

"Pretty good, actually. Are we going to stand here all night jabbering, or are you going to set us free!" Zhu Bajie snapped.

But Sandy wasn't listening. He caught a glimpse of Meilin crouching at Zhu Bajie's feet. His mouth dropped open with surprise.

He made a quick motion with his hand, and the rope net was quickly hoisted back up into the canopy by four of the ninja monkeys.

Sandy then knelt and offered his hand to Meilin. "Please," he said.

Meilin tentatively took Sandy's hand and the monk helped her to rise.

"Could it really be?" Sandy mouthed with wonder.

"Oh yes," Zhu Bajie smiled. "This—is Meilin," he stated proudly.

Immediately, upon hearing her name, all the ninja monkeys dropped to their knees and knelt before her.

"Meilin," Zhu Bajie continued, "This worthless excuse for a demon monk is your uncle, Sha Wujing."

"I haven't seen you since..." Sha Wujing said, forming the size of a tiny infant with his hands.

"I'm very, very honored," he finished, bowing his head.

As tired, frightened and exhausted as she was, Meilin bowed her head in return. She then glanced past Sandy at the ninja monkeys. They still knelt before her, staring at the ground.

"Why are they kneeling?" she asked.

Sha Wujing looked questioningly at Zhu Bajie.

"She sort'a just discovered herself a few hours ago. Hasn't sunk in yet," Zhu Bajie remarked casually.

"Oh," Sha Wujing nodded. He then turned his attention back to Meilin. "These warriors serve your father. Therefore they serve you—Princess."

"Princess?" Meilin coughed.

"Indeed," Sha Wujing said with a smile. "You *are* the daughter of Sun Wukong, the Monkey King. All of monkey-kind are your subjects."

"Great," Meilin muttered under her breath. There was disappointment in her voice. "Now I'm *Sheena of the Jungle...*"

"Sheena?" Sha Wujing again looked to Zhu Bajie for clarification.

"It's a future thing," Zhu Bajie replied.

"Look," Meilin said, trying to control her frustration. "I don't need subjects and I certainly don't wanna be princess of the monkey kingdom.

I'm here to save my mother and get back to my life!"

"Lijuan's here?" Sha Wujing gasped.

"Yes, well, that's the other thing we need to talk about," Zhu Bajie reluctantly admitted.

Zhu Bajie summarized the events of the past hours to Sha Wujing as the group moved through the dense bamboo forest to the tiny cave the demon monk was using as an outpost to stage his subversive operations.

The cave's narrow entrance was concealed by an outcrop of brush and rock jutting from the ground. Sha Wujing's assignment was to disrupt the demon supply lines to the Heavenly Palace as much as possible.

Meilin used the time that passed for her uncle's long-winded explanation to find her Tao and revert to her human form.

"This is grave news, indeed. Sun Wukong and the Jade Emperor need to know at once!" Sha Wujing stated firmly after Zhu Bajie concluded his story inside the cramped quarters of the cave.

"My father's nearby?" Meilin asked.

"No," Sha Wujing answered. "Your father's been secretly traveling on behalf of the Jade Emperor to enlist the rulers of animal-kind not completely loyal to Bull King, to support the Celestial Army in a bid to rout the demon from the Heavenly

Palace. Once the Emperor reestablishes his throne, we can work on driving Bull King back to the Underworld where he belongs. It's been difficult. Most are aligned with the Underworld out of fear. But if we can somehow retake the Palace, we can break the hold he has on them. But now, with your mother in his hands..." Sha Wujing shook his head with a measure of defeat.

"What do you mean?" Meilin demanded.

"Once your father learns Bull King has Lijuan, he'll do anything it takes to save her—including surrendering. And without your Father to lead the Celestial forces, I'm afraid all is lost."

"But we can't leave my mother in Bull King's hands!" Meilin cried.

"No, we can't. And we can't keep this news from your father, either," Sha Wujing said, scratching his chin in thought.

A shrill bird-like whistle broke the moment. Within seconds, one of the ninja monkeys dropped down into the cave. He bowed once to Meilin and then turned to Sha Wujing.

"The scout returns," he grunted in a rough monkey voice.

Sha Wujing rose and motioned Meilin and Zhu Bajie to follow him. The three exited the cave and waited.

Zhu Bajie and Meilin concealed themselves from sight in the brush. Sha Wujing stood in the open by a thick bamboo grove.

It was now early dawn. The rising sun filtered its light through the bamboo canopy, warming the cold forest with a green-yellow glow.

A lone reddish-grey fox soon appeared, running silently on all fours, straight for their position. Twenty feet before them, the fox stopped and morphed itself into a woman-like demon fox—a Huli-jing. She was actually quite beautiful, Meilin thought—in a demon-fox kind of way.

She was straightforward and direct. "Patrols are scouring the towns, looking for two people. A big fat pig and his companion—possibly a young girl. A reward of 20,000 gold pieces is offered for any information leading to their capture."

"Big fat pig?" Zhu Bajie objected indignantly as he stood. "Well, I never!"

"Easy, Pigsy," Sha Wujing cautioned.

Meilin also stood. The demon-fox raised her eyebrows at Meilin's sudden appearance.

"So, it's true," she said. She then bowed slightly and reached into her jacket.

The sound of swift cold steel drawn against scabbards warned the Huli-jing to withdraw her hand slowly. But the demon-fox wasn't perturbed by the ninja monkeys that placed their bodies protectively in front of Meilin.

Still, she withdrew her hand slowly, holding a tightly rolled paper scroll. With a flick of her wrist, she unfurled it for Sha Wujing to read.

She stepped forward and presented it to him.

"Well, well..." Sha Wujing said, as he scanned the scroll. "The Lantern Festival's still on. Villagers are now required to donate food to the banquet as well as entertainment or risk the consequences."

"Consequences?" Meilin asked.

"Seems we've been doing our job a little too well. If there are any more attacks on Bull King's supply lines, villages will be burned and prisoners will be taken and held accountable."

"You mean killed..." Meilin said gravely.

"Yes," Sha Wujing replied.

Meilin turned and walked a short distance away from her two uncles and sat down. Her shoulders shook slightly.

Zhu Bajie knew she was crying. The emotional strain was too much for her. Zhu Bajie motioned for Sha Wujing to stay put and lumbered to Meilin's side. He lowered his massive bulk and sat beside her.

"What kind of awful world is this?" Meilin said, wiping her face.

"It's not," Zhu Bajie replied. "It's the place of legend and storybook heroes you grew up with as a child—a beautiful and magical world that's come under the spell of Darkness."

"No," Meilin said, shaking her head. "In those stories, the heroes always won."

"True," Zhu Bajie agreed. "But those stories have already been written. This one—*your* story—hasn't."

Meilin eyed her uncle. "What if my story has an unhappy ending?"

"What if it doesn't?" Zhu Bajie returned.

Meilin exhaled. "This isn't going to be another one of your *'glass-half-empty, glass-half-filled'* sermons, is it?"

"Does it need to be?" Zhu Bajie said.

"No," Meilin answered. Then she added, "Any chance of skipping ahead to see how it ends? Because from where I sit, all I can see is *no-talent Monkey-girl screws up and gets everyone killed.*"

"Afraid not," Zhu Bajie said. "Besides, who says you have no talent? You're Sun Wukong's daughter. You have more talent than you know. We just gotta find a way to bring it to life."

"Uncle Z," Meilin interrupted, "I'm just a scared little California girl with a monkey tail."

"And your father was the biggest troublemaker the Jade Emperor ever knew until he gained

Enlightenment. Now, he's the Heavenly Kingdom's only hope. And, your mother's! Are you telling me that you don't think there's anything you can do, even if it's just simply to pray?"

A single tear trickled down Meilin's cheek. Zhu Bajie was right—as usual. Her mind raced. If she did nothing, her mother would die. Yet, if she did something—something wrong, her mother could die as well. The glass-half-empty scenario was a losing proposition any way she looked at it.

"Who can teach me what I need to know?" she said with resolve.

Zhu Bajie beamed and stood. He lifted Meilin to her feet.

"A lot of people," Zhu Bajie said. "And, if you had 500 years to study, you might learn a thing or two. What we need is someone who can awaken what you inherited at birth—now! And there's only one person who can do the job."

"Who?" Meilin asked anxiously.

"Your father!"

Chapter 8

"**N**o one's allowed access to the inner court. And certainly, no one sees his Imperial Majesty, the Jade Emperor, without an appointment. No one!" an indignant weasel-faced courtier said, dismissing Zhu Bajie without so much as looking at him. "Now, if I were you, I'd take your big fat rump and your dirty little servant and get out of here before I have you removed. Frankly, I don't even know how you got in..."

"Really..." Zhu Bajie said calmly. He then reached up and grabbed the surly low-level courtier by his long scraggly chin hair and yanked his face close to his.

"We just traveled three thousand years through time and another 1000 leagues on a cloud to get to this lousy makeshift excuse for a royal palace and you're telling me that the Jade Emperor has no time to see the great Zhu Bajie—former General of the Heavenly River and Commander of over 800,000 naval soldiers?"

The weasel-faced courtier winced in pain as Zhu Bajie twisted the thin man's whiskers in his hand. "That's exactly what I'm telling you," he grimaced, standing his ground. "Besides, everyone knows Zhu Bajie disappeared 14 years ago in the great battle. So next time, pick a name that might work!" The courtier pulled his beard free from Zhu Bajie's grip.

"We have important news that concerns his Majesty and Sun Wukong!"

"So does every *mao* and *gou* that comes here wanting something. Put it in a letter and if I think it's worth a toot, I'll schedule you for next month."

Zhu Bajie's face turned beet-red. He motioned for Meilin to step aside.

"Pig-style?" Meilin asked.

"Pig-style!" Zhu Bajie replied.

- - -

Inside the inner chamber, the Jade Emperor and his generals were discussing war strategy. His generals moved blocks of carved clay soldiers around a huge tiled floor map of the Heavenly Kingdom, while the bored Emperor looked on.

Suddenly, the doors to the chamber were blown inward off their hinges with a tremendous *BANG* caused by the flying body of the wailing weasel-faced courtier. He landed with a thud in the center of the floor map, scattering the battle pieces everywhere.

Instantly, the generals pulled their swords and placed themselves in front of their monarch, ready for what they assumed was a surprise attack by demon assassins.

Instead, Zhu Bajie strolled into the chamber like he owned the place, his nine-toothed rake slung over his shoulder, idly flicking dust from his robe.

Meilin followed a few feet behind.

The weasel-faced courtier scrambled to his knees and kowtowed at the Emperor's feet. "I tried to keep him out..."

"Zhu Bajie!" the Jade Emperor proclaimed with astonishment.

"Zhu Bajie?" the courtier whined and stammered. "But—but..."

The Jade Emperor pushed past the groveling courtier and his generals.

"Your Majesty," Zhu Bajie said flatly. "We need to talk."

The Jade Emperor ordered the room cleared with a wave of his hand. Two of his generals had to drag the still-apologizing courtier away by his feet.

The Jade Emperor shook his head. His face was drawn and weary from the years of living in hunted exile.

"I'm surrounded by buffoons," he said, bending down and picking up one of the clay battle pieces and staring at it. "My army's weak. For every skirmish we win, we lose three. What possible news could you bring to make things worse?"

"Lijuan's been captured!" Zhu Bajie said heavily.

The Jade Emperor hung his head. He tossed the clay battle piece back to the tiled floor map. It shattered to pieces when it hit the floor.

"So... It's over then," he said. "Bull King has won. Thank you, Zhu Bajie. You may go."

The Jade Emperor turned away, lost in thought.

"GO?" Meilin cried. She tugged on Zhu Bajie's sleeve, demanding his attention. "Uncle Z, you said this old goat could help us!"

"Old goat?" the Jade Emperor growled. There was immeasurable anger in his voice as he spun around and glared at Meilin. "Is this how you train your servants?" he spat at Zhu Bajie. "Does she even know what will happen to her for speaking such insult?"

"Let's go, Uncle Z," Meilin said, ignoring the Jade Emperor. "This guy's no ruler. He's a waste of time."

Meilin turned and began walking toward the broken chamber doors. After a few steps, she stopped and turned back to the Jade Emperor. "You know, we have a name for people like you back where I come from—it's *lose-ah!*" Meilin emphasized the word "lose-ah" by holding up her hand and making the "L" sign near her forehead. "Thanks for nothing! We'll find my father ourselves. He'll know what to do to save Mom!"

Zhu Bajie smiled at the Jade Emperor and shrugged an apology, "Kids... What'cha gonna do?"

Zhu Bajie also turned his back on the Jade Emperor and began to leave.

"Wait!" the Jade Emperor called. "Father? Mother?" He then took a good look at Meilin. "This isn't..."

"Oops—my bad. I forgot to make the introductions," Zhu Bajie replied to the stunned monarch. "Your Majesty, this is Meilin, the Monkey King's daughter."

- - -

Meilin sat and waited patiently for nearly two hours while Zhu Bajie brought the Jade Emperor up to speed on the events that spanned the past day. The only upside to reliving the tale was that the Jade Emperor ordered his servants to bring food—which Zhu Bajie, being true to his nature, consumed rather like a pig.

Meilin and Zhu Bajie were given quarters on the second floor of the abandoned ancient stone monastery the Jade Emperor and his court had taken refuge in.

Meilin ate sparingly. Though she was famished, she just didn't have an appetite. She was worried about her mother and what she must be going through. Was Lijuan locked in a rat-infested cell, or chained to a wall in some dark and dirty dungeon? Or worse?

Meilin had seen enough sword and sorcery films on cable TV to imagine what it might be like. The prospects sent a shiver down her spine, because what was happening now wasn't a movie. It was real!

"Lijuan's capture couldn't come at a worse time," the Jade Emperor said. "Bull King and his demon army caught us completely off-guard when he attacked 14 years ago. For the past two years, we've been planning a little surprise of our own. But everything hinges on Sun Wukong's ability to gather the support we need from the Animal Kings. Without them—and without Sun Wukong to lead them—I'm afraid we'll never regain the Heavenly Palace or restore Balance."

"I'm a bit mystified how Bull King was able to pull it off in the first place. He's not the brightest cow in the pasture," Zhu Bajie remarked. "And how did he activate the Gate? He's powerful, but not *that* powerful."

"He has help," the Jade Emperor replied.

Zhu Bajie turned from his dinner and focused his attention on the weary monarch.

"Xiang Yao," the Jade Emperor said.

Zhu Bajie stopped chewing. "Xiang Yao! But he was cast down by the Eight Immortals eons ago!"

"Who's Xiang Yao?" Meilin asked, her interest suddenly piqued.

"A sorcerer demon," Zhu Bajie replied. "He serves Yanluo—the God of Death, whom your father once tricked when he entered the Fourth Hell and removed his name from the Book of the Dead."

"The only way for Yanluo to save face and strip your father of his immortality is for Sun Wukong to rewrite his name in the Book," the Jade Emperor added.

"And he'd do that?" Meilin asked.

"To save your mother," Zhu Bajie said, "he would!"

One of the Jade Emperor's retainers, a cat-faced demon, entered the chamber. He bowed once and presented a rolled scroll nested atop a blue cushion.

The Jade Emperor took the scroll and motioned for the attendant to leave. He then unfurled the scroll and read it.

"It's official," he said heavily. "Bull King's demanding Sun Wukong surrender himself at the Heavenly Palace during the culmination of the Lantern Festival, or Lijuan will be put to death."

"NO!" Meilin screamed and bolted to her feet. "Uncle Z! What can we do?" Meilin was beset with both rage and terror. Her human form instantly and automatically morphed into its monkey state. This time the transition was complete. She went full monkey.

The Jade Emperor's jaw dropped at what he saw.

"We need to do something right now!" Meilin demanded, not aware of what just happened.

"Easy!" Zhu Bajie said. "We will. Center yourself, Meilin!"

Meilin paused long enough in her rage to look at herself—her arms, her legs, her face.

"AHH!" she screamed in utter frustration. She ran from the room to the terrace outside.

"Give us a moment," Zhu Bajie said, standing. He left the Jade Emperor and went after Meilin. He found her huddled in a secluded corner of the terrace, clawing at her skin, trying to rip the fur off her arm.

"What good is this monkey stuff if I can't do anything!" she wailed, fighting Zhu Bajie's attempts to keep her from hurting herself. "I hate it! I hate it! I wish I was never born!"

"No! Never say that!" Zhu Bajie cried, holding Meilin as tightly as he could, while she completely broke down. Tears streamed down her face.

"If I was never born, my mother wouldn't be in this mess! And my father would have never left her! It's all my fault! And there's nothing I can do!"

"Meilin," a soft voice said. A radiating light from above washed over Meilin and Zhu Bajie. Through her watery eyes, Meilin could see the semblance of an extraordinarily beautiful woman materialize, hovering above the ground.

Zhu Bajie instantly spun on his knees and bowed low, touching his forehead to the ground.

"Guanyin," he said with great respect in his voice.

It was Meilin's grandmother, Guanyin, Goddess of Mercy. Her ethereal form floated closer. "Do not despair," she said softly, reaching out her hand.

"Everything you need to know is inside here," she said, touching Meilin's forehead. "And here," she said, touching Meilin's heart. "When you believe in yourself—when you find your true inner Tao—your light will shine."

"Grandma?" Meilin said with wonder, reaching up to touch Guanyin. But her hand passed through the Goddess as she floated back and faded away.

"Don't go! I don't understand! I need you to teach me!" Meilin's words echoed across the empty terrace. Guanyin was gone.

Zhu Bajie raised himself to a sitting position.

"Was that really her? Meilin asked. "Was that my grandmother?"

"Yes," Zhu Bajie said, taking Meilin's hand and helping her to stand. "Now, what say we dry those eyes and come back inside."

"Take your hands off my daughter!" an angry voice commanded.

Zhu Bajie turned and looked. "Sun Wukong!"

It was Monkey King!

"Traitor!" Sun Wukong snapped. "You promised to protect my family with your life, yet here you are, still breathing!"

"Wukong, forgive me!" Zhu Bajie said dropping to his knees before the incensed Monkey King. "I've failed you!"

Sun Wukong spun Ru Yi Jin Gu Bang, his magic golden-clasped rod, in his hands and smashed it across Zhu Bajie's face, sending the demon pig flying across the terrace, crashing into a stone wall. The stone wall crumbled from the force and large pieces of rock fell atop Zhu Bajie.

Sun Wukong didn't wait for Zhu Bajie to recover. Before Zhu Bajie even rolled over, Sun Wukong was on him. He lifted the huge pig off the ground like a rag-doll and began bludgeoning him mercilessly with his rod.

"Stop!" Meilin cried. "You're killing him!"

But Sun Wukong wasn't listening. He was relentless in the bone-shattering punishment he dealt. Zhu Bajie offered no resistance. He had failed to keep his promise to protect Meilin and Lijuan. If death was the consequence for failure, he accepted it.

Sun Wukong raised his staff for a killing blow. As Ru Yi Jin Gu Bang descended, Meilin snapped. In a flash she flew across the terrace in a single leap, unconsciously pulling the longest of her three hair sticks from her hair. Instantly the jade hair stick grew to bo-staff size.

She intercepted the descending blow of Sun Wukong's magic rod and stopped it inches from obliterating Zhu Bajie's skull.

Meilin then whirled into action and drove Sun Wukong back with relentless fury. Her jade bo-staff spun with the expertise of a master. Sun Wukong easily parried his daughter's blows and let her continue to attack him. With each thrust, Meilin became stronger and stronger, until she was no longer thinking, but acting on pure instinct.

"Enough!" Sun Wukong commanded, suddenly sweeping Meilin off her feet and pinning her to the ground with Ru Yi Jin Gu Bang.

Meilin glared up at him. "I hate you!" she spat, as she wriggled free. She rolled to her feet and ran to Zhu Bajie. She grabbed her uncle's battered face and hugged him. His face was swollen and discolored.

"HATE YOU!" she screamed again.

"Meilin!" Sun Wukong returned. "I *am* your father!"

"No you're not!" Meilin cried. "Uncle Z's been more of a father to me than you'll ever be. My real father would never do this! You're a monster!"

"Meilin," Zhu Bajie said, wincing with pain. "Stop! Center..."

"But?" Meilin said with surprise in her voice.

Zhu Bajie held up his hand for assistance, but to Sun Wukong, not Meilin. "You didn't have to hit me so hard," he griped.

"I had to make it look real, otherwise she never would have reached inside herself," Sun Wukong said as he stepped forward and hauled Zhu Bajie to his feet.

"But..." Meilin stammered again.

"Meilin," Zhu Bajie said, turning to her. "If your father really wanted to kill me, he would have done so on the first blow."

"Believe me, I thought about it," Sun Wukong stated. "You did fail me."

"It wasn't his fault," Meilin interjected boldly. "I—opened the Gate."

Sun Wukong nodded, spreading his arms wide, inviting his daughter to come to him. The gesture melted Meilin's heart and she ran to his open arms.

"Father!" she cried and hugged him with fourteen years of pent-up frustration and love. Sun Wukong returned Meilin's embrace with equal fervor.

"I'm so sorry I couldn't be with you," Sun Wukong said. "But it was the only option we had. You—are everything to us. And if it meant that I'd never see you grow up, it was a small price to pay."

"But what about Mom?" Meilin blurted out. "How can we save her?"

"I don't know," Sun Wukong replied. "But one thing is certain—I *will* present myself to Bull King on Lantern Festival's Eve."

"But he'll kill you!"

Sun Wukong snorted. "I'm immortal, remember?"

"No!" Meilin replied. "He's got a sorcerer. They're gonna make you rewrite your name in the Book of the Dead."

"Eh-heh-heh," Sun Wukong laughed, in his monkey way. "If that's what it takes to free your mother—so be it. Besides, no one should live forever. Not even an immortal."

Chapter 9

"He's gone, isn't he," Meilin said, as the Sun rose over the mountainous horizon. She'd rested all night in her father's arms on the terrace, the two of them gazing at the stars in the heavens above. They didn't say much to each other. They didn't need to. Simply being close to each other was enough. Meilin didn't want that moment to ever end, but it did. She didn't remember finally falling asleep either, but she did.

It was just before sunrise when Sun Wukong rose, kissed Meilin once on her head and silently slipped away.

Her statement to Zhu Bajie didn't require an answer. Meilin knew her father had already made his decision.

"You didn't have to trick me last night," Meilin said, now turning to face her uncle, who sat on the floor behind her.

"Yes, we did," Zhu Bajie said, holding a large block of ice on his still aching head. "There needed to be a way that you would believe what your grandmother told you. Anger seemed to be the best way. Every time you become agitated, you go Monkey. It's your built-in defense mechanism. Otherwise it might have taken years of training to evoke what you inherited at birth."

"And what exactly did I inherit?

"Who knows? His magic? His knowledge of the 72 Transformations? His strength? His fighting ability?"

"His immortality?"

"No," Zhu Bajie said with confidence. "That's something that's granted—or pilfered in your father's case. So you need to be careful. You can be hurt—maybe even killed."

"Okay then," Meilin said, standing. She went outside to the terrace.

"Which way is it to the Heavenly Palace?" she asked.

"Why?" Zhu Bajie said, joining her.

"Because I'm not sitting here doing nothing while my father sacrifices himself again. Now, how do I conjure up one of those cloud thingies?"

"Well, you just sort'a swirl your hand like this and—wait a minute!" Zhu Bajie said as Meilin began the invocation. "Can't we at least have breakfast first?"

"Get a doggie bag!" Meilin replied as a small cloud formed at her feet. It lifted her off the ground. "Cool!" she remarked, pleased with herself.

"What do I say to get this puppy going? Up-up and away?"

"If you want," Zhu Bajie smiled. "Usually, I just think it..."

But Meilin was already on her way.

"Hey! Wait for me!" Zhu Bajie called, conjuring his own cloud and chasing after her. "Those things come with a learner's permit, you know!"

Within a few moments, Zhu Bajie caught up to her. He could see the exhilaration on Meilin's face as she soared across the morning sky, hundreds of feet above ground.

"You know, with one of these, I'd never be late for schoo... Ach! Ooooo Bug! I swallowed a bug!" she choked.

Zhu Bajie laughed out loud. "Oh yeah. I forgot to mention... Keep your mouth closed."

"A little late with the info, don't ya think!" Meilin gacked.

Zhu Bajie smiled and shrugged, sorry.

It was noon when they touched down in the bamboo forest near Sha Wujing's hidden camp. The demon monk was happy to see them again.

"What happened to you?" Sha Wujing asked, noticing Zhu Bajie's lumpy face.

"I ran into a wall," Zhu Bajie replied.

"Hmph!" Sha Wujing countered. "I'd say the wall ran into you."

"Ha-Ha..." Zhu Bajie grunted.

"Uncle Sha," Meilin interrupted. "We need a way into the Heavenly Palace without being seen."

Sha Wujing stared at her with raised eyebrows. "You're joking, of course."

"She's not," Zhu Bajie said. "We need to get in there before the Festival ends. Lijuan's life—and Wukong's, might depend upon it!"

Sha Wujing returned his attention to Meilin and could see that she was indeed dead serious. He stroked his chin while he thought.

"Impossible..." he frowned. "Everyone entering the Palace for the Festival is being thoroughly searched. Everyone except..."

Sha Wujing turned to one of his monkey ninja warriors. "That small caravan you reported on last night. Where is it now?"

"At a standard marching pace, it should pass through the northwest ravine within the hour," the monkey warrior grunted.

"Assemble the men!" Sha Wujing ordered.

The ninja monkey turned and made a gruff monkey hoot. Within seconds, a contingent of thirty warriors assembled, armed and set for action.

"We're ready," he said, turning back to Sha Wujing.

Sha Wujing nodded and scanned his men. "Protect the Princess at all costs!"

The ninja monkeys acknowledged the command with a firm monkey grunt as they saluted Sha Wujing with open hands covering clenched fists.

"They'll escort you," Sha Wujing said to Meilin.

"Can't we fly?" Meilin asked, eager to take to the sky again.

"Too risky. We might be spotted," Sha Wujing replied. "The canopy offers the best cover in case we run into a patrol. Don't worry. They won't drop you."

"Who's worried?" Meilin stated, morphing from her human form into her monkey form—but without the tail. She already decided she didn't care for that.

"It's time I got to know my father's side of the family," Meilin said with a smile. With a quick leap, she launched herself up into the bamboo canopy. The ninja monkeys quickly followed.

"See if you can keep up with us!" she called to her uncles below. The ninja monkeys then took off, speeding through the canopy, leaping from branch to branch—Meilin gliding right along with them. Meilin felt exhilarated as she effortlessly kept pace. It was as much fun as flying.

"That's not the terrified little girl I first met two days ago," Sha Wujing observed as Meilin disappeared from view.

"Oh, it's the same girl, all right," Zhu Bajie replied. "Still terrified—but now—she's mad!"

- - -

They didn't have long to wait before a column of slow-moving wagons under demon guard appeared on the rocky road that cut through the ravine. This was the last point of land that offered any cover before the terrain gave way to several miles of tall grass-covered moguls and open field. Shortly thereafter, the fields melted into the pure billowy cloud that surrounded the Heavenly Palace like an endless moat, suspended far above the valleys below.

The caravan was composed of fifteen flatbed wagons laden with baskets of food and barrels of wine extorted from the surrounding villages. Lagging behind at the end of the caravan was a rickety red gypsy wagon, pulled by an old water buffalo that could barely keep pace with the rest of the column. The words *The Great Qilin* and *Bian Lian* were painted in large yellow letters on the ornate sideboards.

"Well-well-well," Zhu Bajie remarked, watching from behind the cover of rock and scrub. "That one!" he pointed.

"Why that one?" Sha Wujing said. "We can easily take the entire caravan."

"And then what? March in with your ninja monkeys posing as Demon guards?" Zhu Bajie snorted. "We wouldn't get past the main gate."

Sha Wujing reluctantly agreed. "Do you need a distraction?"

Zhu Bajie shook his head. "No. We'll have to do this one quietly."

As soon as the caravan passed their position, Zhu Bajie signaled Meilin to ready herself.

"Follow me, and no matter what—don't make a sound," he said.

Meilin nodded, still unsure as to what her uncle was up to. He then signaled two of the ninja monkeys to ready themselves, as well.

As soon as the front of the column was out of site, Zhu Bajie was on his feet and ran up to the rear of the trailing entertainer's wagon. The two ninja monkeys and Meilin followed in single file, careful not to stray from the gypsy wagon's centerline, in case a demon soldier might chance to look back.

Zhu Bajie latched onto the rear wooden steps of the entertainer's wagon, hauled his massive bulk up and slipped inside the unlocked rear door.

The lightly dozing Great Qilin woke with surprise as Zhu Bajie stepped inside.

"Can I have your autograph?" Zhu Bajie asked. Before Qilin could call out for help, Zhu Bajie clunked him on the head with his nine-toothed rake and tossed his unconscious body out the back of the wagon into the waiting arms of one of the ninja monkeys.

The other ninja monkey then helped Meilin leap up into the wagon as Zhu Bajie went forward and dispatched the driver in a similar manner, tossing him out the rear, as well.

The second ninja monkey took charge of the unconscious driver and disappeared back into the brush.

Zhu Bajie then morphed himself into the driver and took his place at the reins.

"Now what?" Meilin said in a low voice.

"Sit back and enjoy the ride," Zhu Bajie replied. "And while you're back there, see if there's anything to eat! All that running made me hungry!"

Meilin rolled her eyes at her uncle's request and rummaged through the cart. "Nothing here except a bunch of fancy silk costumes," Meilin said, looking through The Great Qilin's wardrobe.

"Try them on," Zhu Bajie whispered.

"Why?"

"'Cause there's no business like show business," Zhu Bajie said. "And be quick about it. We'll be at the Main Gate to the Heavenly Palace soon!"

Meilin shrugged and did what her uncle asked. She picked through The Great Qilin's costumes, looking for something that might fit.

"What does this guy do?" she asked, as she found something purple and green that seemed to be her size.

Zhu Bajie didn't answer.

Meilin held up the silk vest for a closer look— and spotted a wooden trunk under the man's bed.

Meilin knelt and slid it out. The trunk was heavy, but it wasn't locked.

Meilin lifted the lid.

"Whoa!" she remarked with surprise when she saw what was inside.

- - -

It was mid-afternoon when the caravan was waved through the Main Gate to the Heavenly

Palace without inspection, just as Zhu Bajie anticipated.

They were stopped, however, by two ugly-looking, cow-faced demons several yards inside the wide cobblestone promenade that led toward the Central Square—the most likely spot where Bull King would later appear for the culmination of the Festival.

"Yo! Fatso!" the larger of the two demons shouted.

Zhu Bajie pulled back on his water buffalo's reins and smiled dumbly at the Demon.

"Entertainers—that way!" he ordered, pointing down a narrow side street that wound its way around the back of the nearby square.

Zhu Bajie smiled and nodded, jerking the reins and getting the exhausted water buffalo to move again.

"Fatso?" Zhu Bajie muttered, once Qilin's gypsy wagon was out of earshot. "Why does everyone keep saying that?"

Inside the wagon, Meilin giggled. It felt good to laugh, even if it was only for a second. Her stomach was in a knot with worry. Sure, she and Uncle Z had gotten inside the Heavenly Palace, but what next? How would any of this help free her mother. Meilin could see from the curtained windows of the wagon that the Heavenly Palace was full of demon soldiers—probably thousands. What could the two of them do against odds like that? And what if she and Uncle Z were captured themselves? What would happen to her mother then?

Presently Zhu Bajie pulled the gypsy wagon to a stop. He set the wheel brake and came inside, closing the driver's door behind him.

"We're parked near the rear of the Central Square," he said. "There's a large dais constructed in front of the main terrace leading up to the Jade Emperor's Palace. Seems like the focus of interest. When it gets dark, we'll work our way closer."

Suddenly, there was a loud knock on the rear door. Meilin's heart jumped.

"Open up!" a loud voice commanded.

Zhu Bajie motioned for Meilin to remain still and not panic. He went to the rear door and cracked it open.

"Yes?" he said meekly, peering out slightly. It was another sour cow-faced demon, this one with a quill pen and parchment in hand.

"Qilin the Great?" he grunted.

"That's *The Great Qilin*," Zhu Bajie corrected with an exaggerated theatrical voice. "And he's indisposed."

"Whatever!" the demon growled dismissively as he scanned his program schedule. "Tell him he goes on at Sunset. After that, the jugglers—then the dancing bears. Bull King concludes the Festival by vanquishing his greatest enemy—proclaims himself Supreme Ruler of everything, yadda-yadda—cue the fireworks—then we all go home. Got that?"

"Yes," Zhu Bajie said, then added, "But no."

"No?" the demon spat.

"Yes." Zhu Bajie countered.

"Hey, which is it? Yes or no?" the now flustered demon said.

"Both!" Zhu Bajie replied. "Yes, I got it. And no, we won't perform unless we go on last."

"Last?" the demon cow complained. "But my schedule says..."

"Tut-tut, my good demon," Zhu Bajie interrupted. "The Great Qilin *always* performs last. It's in our contract! Do you want to see it? It's signed by Bull King's Secretary of Ceremonial Affairs."

The demon shook his head. Zhu Bajie knew the dumb cow wouldn't question a high official's contract.

"And one more thing," Zhu Bajie added, just to drive his ruse home. "Our contract specifically states that The Great Qilin is to have a basket of grapes and three dozen jelly cakes delivered to his dressing room upon arrival. We're here, and I don't see any grapes or jelly cakes."

The demon cow slapped himself on the head with his hand in frustration. "Look, Fatso. Tell The Great Qilin he can go on last. As for the jelly cakes, get them yourself!"

The demon then stomped away. "Crazy theater people!" he grunted. "Drive me nuts..."

Zhu Bajie frowned and shut the door to the wagon.

"Again with the *Fatso*," Zhu Bajie griped. "Three dozen jelly cakes was probably too much. I bet I could'a had him deliver if I only asked for two..." Zhu Bajie stopped short, gazing at Meilin.

She was as white as a sheet. Zhu Bajie quickly came and sat next to her.

"I'm scared, Uncle Z," she said shivering slightly. Zhu Bajie grabbed the blanket on the bed and put it around her shoulders to keep her warm.

"Me too," he admitted. "Me too..."

Chapter 10

On the royal terrace overlooking the dais, Bull King, wearing full battle armor, sat on the Jade Emperor's throne. He ordered it removed from the Jade Emperor's ceremonial chambers earlier that morning and placed on display for all to see. He wanted it to be very clear to everyone attending the Lantern Festival that he was Ruler Supreme of the Heavenly Kingdom.

To his left stood his sorcerer, Xiang Yao, a vile-looking pale-skinned demon with glowing green eyes and a gaunt skeletal face.

To his right, secured to a massive block of stone by a heavy chain attached to a thick iron collar around her neck, was Lijuan.

Meilin could not see her mother from where their gypsy wagon was parked. Zhu Bajie ordered her to remain inside the wagon with the curtains closed until he returned. He wanted to assess the situation firsthand, before plotting a course of action.

So far, he hadn't come up with anything workable—a detail he definitely wouldn't confide to Meilin. It was a long run up the steps from the dais to the terrace where Bull King sat in review of the festivities. A lot could happen in that time—including killing Lijuan.

The Central Square was crowded with drunken soldiers and a mixture of other demon-kind allied with Bull King's forces, including diplomats, soldiers and simple spectators.

Bull King pulled out all stops to make this Lantern Festival the most visually spectacular in recent times. No expenses were spared, from the thousands of colorful lanterns that were hung everywhere—to the food, the entertainment and even the stone statues of himself that were strategically placed throughout, so that no matter which direction one turned, there was always an image of him on display. Everything was designed to proclaim his greatness.

"Hey, Fatso!" a familiar voice grunted. It was the cow-faced demon in charge of stage management.

Zhu Bajie grit his teeth at the word *Fatso*, but wore a happy smile when he turned.

"Oh, there you are," Zhu Bajie grinned, comically setting his hands on his hips. "Did you bring our jelly cakes? You did, didn't you?"

"No, I didn't bring your blasted jelly cakes!" the demon growled. "The jugglers are done. The dancing bears are up and you're next. Tell the Great what's-his-name to get ready! I don't want any screw-ups. Got it?"

"Well... If you say so," Zhu Bajie snorted with feigned exasperation. "But just between you and me, the jelly cake thing was almost a deal-breaker. It took me all afternoon just to smooth things over. I mean, Qilin was ready to walk. But don't worry, I fixed it *just* for you!"

The cow-faced demon stared at Zhu Bajie with his mouth open in disbelief. "Just be ready, okay?" He then spun on his hooves and walked away, shaking his head. "They don't pay me enough for this," he muttered.

Zhu Bajie hurried back to the gypsy wagon and knocked once, then twice, signaling Meilin that he was the one opening the rear wagon door.

"Did you see Mom?" Meilin demanded.

"Yes. She looks okay," Zhu Bajie reassured her. "She's chained to a pillar at the top of the steps leading up from the dais. So we need to alter your act so we can get closer. Once you get started, work your way off the dais and up the steps. I'll follow. When we get close enough to your mom, I'll make my move. It'll be risky, but I think we can time it right. I'll toss a bunch of smoke-balls around, free her, do a little Pig-fu—then we jump on a cloud and hightail it outta here."

"What about Dad?"

"We need to pull this off before he gets here," Zhu Bajie said. "Otherwise, everyone will be on alert and we'll never get the chance."

"I can't do it!" Meilin said, suddenly panicking. The Great Qilin's headdress and face mask shook in her trembling hands. "I can't!"

"Yes—you can!" Zhu Bajie reassured Meilin with a stern voice. "You've seen it done before, right?"

"Once—on a Chinese New Year's DVD!" Meilin countered.

"Okay then," Zhu Bajie replied, as if watching Bian Lian once on a DVD was enough to learn a skill that took a lifetime to perfect. "Piece of cake, right? If you start to mess up, just do a lot of flashy arm-waving and twirling around—anything to keep everyone's eyes on you."

There was a hard knock on the gypsy wagon's rear door.

"Yo, Fatso! Three minutes! Let's go!" It was the voice of the Demon stage manager.

"I *really* don't like that guy!" Zhu Bajie muttered. He then focused his eyes on Meilin. "You can do this," he insisted.

Meilin opened her mouth to protest.

Zhu Bajie raised his finger, silencing her. "You-can-do-this!" he repeated again with all the sincerity he could muster. "Center. Find your Tao. Let all things become one. And no matter what happens—believe in yourself." Then he softened and hugged Meilin.

"Now, put on your mask. And let's go get your mom!"

There were tears of apprehension in Meilin's eyes, but she nodded, took a breath and slipped on her mask.

The demon stage manager was waiting for them outside the wagon when Zhu Bajie threw open the rear door and stepped out with Meilin in tow.

"*This*—is The Great Qilin?" the Demon cow remarked. He then snorted. "Somehow, I'd thought you'd be taller."

"Never speak to The Great Qilin before he goes on!" Zhu Bajie warned. "It's bad luck!"

"Yeah-yeah," the demon grumbled. "Follow me. You're next. And you better be good."

The demon stage manager led Zhu Bajie and Meilin to the performers' waiting area just to the side of the dais where a small group of musicians sat. It was their job to provide music for the performers as needed.

"All right, the bears are coming off," the demon said. "Get ready!"

Zhu Bajie looked at Meilin. She took a deep breath and nodded. It was now or never.

As Meilin placed her foot on the bottom step of the short staircase at the base of the dais, the sound of battle horns from the distant towers interrupted.

On the terrace above, Bull King stood and turned his attention to the darkening sky. He snorted heavily. "Wukong!"

In the distance, Sun Wukong approached, riding on his cloud. He was alone.

The demon stage manager held out his arm, barring Zhu Bajie and Meilin from going any further.

"Sorry, Fatso," the demon grunted. "Looks like you two just got bumped. The main attraction's here."

"But, we have a contract!" Zhu Bajie blustered.

"Take it up with your union!" the demon cow said dismissively. "Grab a seat and enjoy the show!" He then walked away and trotted up the steps of the terrace to get a better look at what was about to happen, himself.

Meilin turned to her uncle. Zhu Bajie could see the absolute terror in her eyes through her mask.

"What do we do?" she cried in a hushed voice.

"I don't know!" Zhu Bajie returned. And he didn't. His plan, having little chance of succeeding in the first place—just went bust.

Sun Wukong flew in fast, landing his cloud in the center of the dais.

All eyes in the Central Square were locked on him, but Sun Wukong only looked at Lijuan. There was nothing but love in his eyes—and anger for her dilemma.

Swords were drawn. The drunken spectators in the Square mooed and bellowed and clamored for Monkey King's blood. Around the upper steps of the terrace, one hundred demon archers appeared and trained their bows on Sun Wukong, ready to let arrows fly if he so much as moved one inch.

Lijuan attempted to descend the steps and go to her husband. But Bull King yanked on the chain around her neck, pulling her back off her feet.

Bull King's roughness angered Sun Wukong, and his golden eyes blazed with fury. But he remained rooted in place, not daring to move.

"Check him!" Bull King grunted, motioning to his sorcerer. Xiang Yao cautiously descended the stone steps and approached Sun Wukong on the dais. In his hand, he held a large crystal shard.

He paused six feet in front of Sun Wukong and held the strange quartz-like shard to his demonic green eyes. He gazed at Sun Wukong through it.

A wicked smile crossed his face. He turned back to Bull King and shouted "It's Wukong! Not a copy!"

Xiang Yao quickly withdrew and returned to the Terrace.

"I'm here!" Sun Wukong said loudly. "Free my wife and let her go!"

"In due time!" Bull King roared. "There's the matter of The Book!"

And with that, the dais upon which Sun Wukong stood, began to change. Xiang Xao directed the stone at Sun Wukong's feet to liquefy and then solidify, locking Monkey King's feet and legs knee-high in solid stone.

Then a terrible dark void materialized on the ground before him, swirling like an inverted tornado that extended down to the very Gates of the Underworld. The air around Monkey King began to swirl, but not sucking him downward— instead, blowing against him.

Out of the swirling vortex, from the depths of Hell, rose The Book of the Dead. The book rotated slowly in space, then stopped. It opened to a blank page, waist-high, in front of Sun Wukong.

"Sign!" Bull King commanded.

Sun Wukong glanced up at Lijuan. She shook her head, begging him not to comply.

"Sign, or she dies *now!*" Bull King roared. Bull King again yanked on Lijuan's chains to reinforce his threat.

Sun Wukong snorted. He reached for the quill pen that rested in the fold of The Book.

Suddenly, there was the CRASH and JINGLE of a tambourine.

"Huli-jing! Demons! Taotie of all ages!" Zhu Bajie shouted from the steps near the side of the dais. "Put your hands together for the world-renowned master of Bian Lian—all the way from Kunlun Mountain—The Great Qilin!"

There was a flash of light and a puff of blue smoke on the dais, and Meilin appeared in full Bian Lian costume.

Zhu Bajie struck up a beat with his tambourine and Meilin began her stylized performance.

"What's going on!" Bull King demanded. His surrounding retainers shook their heads.

The assembled crowd thought it was all part of the show. The group of demon musicians joined in and sweetened the rhythm of Zhu Bajie's tambourine.

Meilin swirled around and began her dance. With every flick of her cloak or the fans she held in her hands that crossed her masked-face, her masks changed in the blink of an eye, thrilling the spectators. Her facemasks went from red, to blue, to green, to yellow, to that of a demon lion, to a frog, to a purple cat—all in rapid-fire succession, mesmerizing everyone.

Everyone except Bull King.

"What's that fool doing!" he growled at the nearby demon stage manager.

"Well, he's..." the cow-faced demon shrugged. "I dunno, but I like it! I mean, how does he do that? Change his face and all."

"Get him off the stage! NOW!" Bull King commanded.

The demon cow nodded and reluctantly strode down the stairs toward Meilin. Zhu Bajie went off-beat with his tambourine signaling Meilin of the danger.

Meilin saw the approaching demon. She twirled herself in front of Sun Wukong, flashed her arms up high, threw down all of her remaining colored smoke balls at her feet, then twirled back to the crowd, revealing her final mask—the face of Bull King.

The crowd went wild and applauded as the Demon stage manager scooped Meilin up and carried her off to the side of the dais.

With order restored, Bull King once again spoke.

"Sign!"

Bull King leveled his war axe and rested its blade on Lijuan's neck. He would tolerate no further delay.

Sun Wukong had no choice. He picked up the quill pen and wrote his name in the Book of the Dead, signing away his immortality forever.

Sun Wukong let the quill drop to the dais.

Bull King smiled and issued the command. "Shoot!"

All one hundred archers let their arrows fly at Sun Wukong. All—hit their mark.

Lijuan screamed in horror. Zhu Bajie dropped his tambourine to the ground and cried "No!"

Meilin stood paralyzed in utter disbelief as her father's head slumped forward. Sun Wukong was dead.

A roaring cheer filled the plaza. Fireworks exploded above. Lijuan crumpled to the terrace sobbing.

Bull King let her restraining chain fall to the ground as he strode triumphantly down the terrace, waving at the crowd.

But as he reached the foot of the dais, he froze. Sun Wukong stirred and lifted his head.

"Eh-heh-heh!" he laughed in his monkey way.

"But?" Bull King spat. "You signed the book!"

"No I didn't!" the Great Qilin said from the side of the dais, making one more quick Bian Lian face change. In a flash, he revealed himself. It was Sun Wukong!

"But?"

"Sun Wukong didn't sign the book!" a defiant voice said.

Bull King's head snapped back to the center of the dais.

Emerging from crouching behind the arrow-riddled Sun Wukong, stood Meilin—the Monkey King's Daughter. The replicant Sun Wukong created when Meilin dropped her smoke balls, dissolved. The arrows that impaled it clattered to the dais.

"So I guess it doesn't count!"

Meilin looked directly at Bull King, held her hand to her forehead in the shape of an 'L' and said, "Lose-ah!"

With that, there was a great roar from the depths of the Underworld. The Book of the Dead burst into flames and was sucked back into the void.

Pandemonium then filled the plaza. Explosions erupted everywhere. From every direction—on foot and from the skies, the Jade Emperor's Heavenly Army attacked. His Celestial forces were overwhelming, bolstered by thousands of Animal Kingdom warriors recruited by Sun Wukong.

The demons in the Square panicked, most too drunk on festival wine to mount an effective defense.

Bull King spun around and shouted up to the terrace, "Kill her!"

The closest demon to Lijuan was the stage manager. He drew his sword, but that was as far as he got. Zhu Bajie, now in his true form, spun him around.

"Remember me?" Zhu Bajie cried.

"Fatso?" the demon stage manager grunted with surprise.

"Yeah," Zhu Bajie replied, clobbering the demon with his nine-toothed rake. "That's for callin' me Fatso!" He then belly-butted the dazed demon, sending him fifty feet into the air, off into a tree. "And that's for not bringing me my jelly cakes!"

Zhu Bajie then spun his rake and shattered the chain binding Lijuan to the pillar. He scooped her up, conjured a cloud and launched her into the night sky where Sha Wujing materialized and whisked her away to safety.

On the dais, the fight was on. Bull King was joined by his elite personal guard who went directly for Sun Wukong—and Meilin.

Immediately, both went into action.

Sun Wukong's magic golden-clasped rod flew into his hands from behind his ear and he leapt into combat, easily dispatching guard after guard, working his way toward Bull King.

Meilin pulled the largest of her three jade hair sticks from her ponytail. It instantly morphed to bo-staff size.

A demon guard came at Meilin and swung his sword at her midsection. Meilin easily sidestepped the blade, spun around and slammed her bo-staff into his ribcage. She then spun the staff up vertically and smashed the demon in his jaw with the rear of the rotating end, sending him instantly to the ground.

Meilin spun and met the next demon's overhead sword attack to her head by sliding a half-step backward and parrying the blow with a downward strike on the demon's wrist with her staff. The demon reversed his blade and cut toward her ribcage. Meilin evaded the slice by quickly shifting her feet and dancing to the left. The demon then brought his sword in an upward arc, which Meilin blocked with her staff, taking another back step. The Demon reversed direction and brought the blade straight down at her head. Meilin easily blocked the blade with her staff.

Locked together, the demon pressed forward with an angry roar, trying to overpower Meilin with his weight, but Meilin simply scooted backward in step with him, causing the Demon to rush forward off-balance. She then half-turned to the left and slapped her staff into the inside of his sword arm with a numbing blow, causing him to drop his blade. Meilin then snapped her staff up and across his face. With a lightning rapid succession of twirls, she then hit the demon in the head, the ribs, down to his left knee, then up to the right side of his head, dropping him where he stood.

Another demon came at Meilin from the rear. Without turning, she spun her staff and reverse-thrust him in his chest with the tip, knocking the wind right out of him. She then arced her staff behind the demon, striking him this time in the back of his neck. She then spun around, faced him, and finished the job with a crack to his knee followed by a fast, downward blow to his head.

More demon soldiers poured onto the dais. Most went to support Bull King, who had his own problems evading Sun Wukong. Wukong was relentless in his fury to pursue him.

Another group of six surrounded Meilin, determined to cut her down.

Meilin spun her jade bo-staff and morphed it back into hair stick size. She poked it back into her ponytail, trading it for the two shorter ones.

These hair sticks instantly morphed into shorter fighting sticks, one for each hand.

One of the six demons rushed in, directing his sword at Meilin's neck. Meilin blocked the sword with her left stick, while jabbing the demon in the throat with her right. She then punched the lower end of her right-handed stick forward into the demon's stomach, and dispatched him with a devastating left hook across the face.

The rest of the five elite demon swordsmen charged in unison. Instead of retreating, Meilin charged also, weaving in and out of them as they tried to cut her down, deflecting each blade with her fighting sticks, alternating left and right, blocking and counter striking. Even as they tried to encircle her, she whirled like a dervish and took all five down in rapid succession with a flurry of precision strikes that could barely be seen.

Meilin spun on her heels, waiting for more to come at her, but the remaining demons on the dais shrank away, wanting no part of her fury.

"I'll mop up here," Zhu Bajie said, joining her. "Go help your Dad!"

Meilin nodded and did a running flip, vaulting over a set of demons foolishly trying to mob Sun Wukong.

"Eh-heh-heh!" Sun Wukong laughed when his daughter landed by his side. Meilin could tell that he was pleased—and proud of her newfound abilities. Meilin was pleased with herself as well. She wasn't afraid. She was fighting alongside someone she'd wanted to know all her life—her father. And what could be better at that moment than being the daughter of the Monkey King!

Bull King, now seeing father and daughter united, retreated up the steps to the terrace overlooking the Square. He summoned more of his demon soldiers already engaged in fighting with Celestial forces on the terrace, to block Sun Wukong and Meilin from following. It was a futile order. It was very clear to Bull King that the day was lost. The Palace was retaken. It was time for him to make his exit.

"Xiang Yao!" he bellowed, calling for his sorcerer.

Xiang Yao materialized by his side, firing bolts of crimson energy from his fingertips in an effort to keep several soldiers of the Wolf and Badger Kingdoms from tearing at his throat.

"Do it now!" Bull King commanded, as Sun Wukong and Meilin gained the top of the steps.

Xiang Yao waved his hands and created a GATE from thin air—a portal by which Bull King could escape to the Underworld.

"He's getting away!" Meilin shouted.

"Eh!" Sun Wukong grunted. He launched himself toward Bull King, flying across the terrace stopping the demon before he could enter Xiang Yao's gate.

The two battled furiously, Bull King's battle axe against Sun Wukong's magic rod. It was no contest. Sun Wukong easily gained the upper hand.

"Xiang Yao!" Bull King cried.

Xiang Yao raised his hands, summoning his demonic bolts. But instead of firing them at Sun Wukong, he crouched and turned, firing them at Meilin.

It was a move Meilin didn't anticipate.

But Sun Wukong did.

Monkey King launched his body in front of his daughter, absorbing the full impact of the energy blast. Being born of stone and immortal, he wasn't affected. But the ensuing explosion and shockwave was all the diversion Bull King needed to step through the void and make his escape.

"THIS ISN'T OVER!" he roared as he vanished.

Xiang Yao followed. The portal closed and disappeared—along with any chance of capturing Bull King—for now...

Sun Wukong rolled to his feet and flicked debris from his breast plate where the bolts hit.

"Hmph!" he spat, disgusted that Bull King eluded him.

Meilin rushed to his side, wrapping her arms around him.

"Are you all right?" she demanded.

"Eh-heh-heh!" Sun Wukong laughed. He hugged his daughter tight.

With their supreme leader gone, the demon army quickly dispersed and fled the Palace into the surrounding mountains. Those who were slower surrendered without further resistance and were disarmed.

The battle was over. The day was won.

Chapter 11

At sunrise the next morning, the Jade Emperor stood on the terrace overlooking the Central Square before the thousands of Celestial and Animal Kingdom soldiers gathered to hear him proclaim victory.

He was surrounded by his generals, courtiers and Celestial advisors. Off to the side, slightly apart from the Imperial Party, stood Sun Wukong, Zhu Bajie, Sha Wujing, Lijuan and Meilin.

"We're gathered here today," the Jade Emperor began, speaking to the assembled throng, "to honor those who have fallen, those who have survived, and those who have sacrificed everything in order to restore Balance and rout the Demon usurper from our Kingdom. It's been fourteen years..."

"Something tells me this is going to be a fourteen-year speech," Sha Wujing whispered.

"No kidding," Zhu Bajie replied. "What say we bail and get something to eat. I'm starving!"

Zhu Bajie, looked at the rest of the group to see if they agreed. They did. The five of them slipped quietly away as the Jade Emperor droned on.

Their path took them through the garden and near the gate Guanyin created to save Lijuan and the infant Meilin.

Lijuan held Sun Wukong's arm as they walked, her head on his shoulder. Meilin walked at her mother's side. Zhu Bajie and Sha Wujing brought up the rear, arguing about food.

As the group walked past the Gate, Meilin paused and stared at it.

The group stopped and waited for her.

"Something wrong?" Lijuan asked. She could see Meilin had something heavy on her mind.

Meilin took a long moment then spoke. "I don't want to stay here. I want to go home..."

"But, *this* is your home," Zhu Bajie said.

"No," she replied. Her voice was hesitant. "I know I was born here. But—I didn't grow up here."

Meilin looked at her parents. "Mom... Dad... It's hard to explain, but I don't feel like I belong. At least, not yet."

Lijuan looked up at Sun Wukong. The Monkey King nodded and smiled.

"We understand," Lijuan said.

"I know I have family here," Meilin continued. "I'm just not ready."

Lijuan and Sun Wukong came to Meilin.

"What would you like to do?" Lijuan asked.

"I don't know," Meilin frowned. "I feel like I'm tearing the family apart again, when I should feel the opposite. I've finally found out who I am, you and Dad are together again, but..."

"The Gate works," Zhu Bajie chimed in. "Who's to say you can't live in both worlds? Or, spend holidays and summer vacations here?"

Sun Wukong exhaled heavily. "I was going to destroy the Gate. But, with Bull King still on the loose..." He turned to Lijuan. "Perhaps it's safer for you both."

Lijuan looked at her husband. He was right. There was still work for him to do. Bull King was at large and in spite of the Jade Emperor's proclamation, this world was *not* in Balance yet.

"We are always and forever," Sun Wukong said lovingly to Lijuan. He then looked at Meilin, "No matter where either of you are."

"Hello..." Zhu Bajie interrupted. "Hungry pig here... The Gate? You can see each other anytime? Now, I'm thinking of a couple of short stacks, a dozen eggs over easy, coffee. Then for breakfast..."

"Uncle Z!" Meilin laughed.

"What?" Zhu Bajie said. He then turned to Sha Wujing. "Do you know that for a couple of bucks, you can go to these places called buffets and eat as much as you want."

"Hmm," Sha Wujing remarked. "What's a buck?"

- - -

It was a bittersweet good-bye.

Meilin unlocked and activated the Gate with her jade hair sticks. She then ran and hugged her father tightly.

"I love you," she said.

"Eh-heh-heh," Sun Wukong laughed in his monkey way, only much softer. He smiled down at his daughter. His golden eyes sparkled. "I love you, too," he said.

Sun Wukong then looked at Zhu Bajie. "Beware Bull King and Xiang Yao!"

Zhu Bajie nodded.

Sun Wukong then took both Meilin and Lijuan's hands and guided them to the open Gate. With one last kiss for Lijuan, he ushered them into the void.

Chapter 12

When Meilin strode into school that morning, all eyes turned her way. She wasn't the nerdy little girl they were used to seeing and ignoring anymore. She walked with a visible confidence that radiated from her entire body. She wore jeans and a simple top—Chinese style. Her long hair was gathered into a ponytail, held in place by her three jade hair sticks.

Even the Tiffany-clones paused and stared. When Jessie saw her, she ran to catch up.

"Hey!" she whispered to her friend. "Did I see what I thought I saw?"

"Yup," Meilin replied as she continued down the hall toward her locker.

The first period bell rang. Jessie's homeroom was in the other direction.

"I'll explain everything tonight!" Meilin said as they parted.

"You better!" Jessie called.

- - -

That afternoon after school, the girls' junior varsity volleyball team met in the gym for their final scrimmage. Interscholastic games were scheduled to start in two days.

It was first-string red against blue.

Tiffany and her posse were confident of another easy win.

"Ready for another lesson, Cheng?" Tiffany taunted.

"Bring it!" Meilin replied.

Tiffany laughed.

Coach Daniels blew her whistle. Red served first. The ball was high and long to the backcourt. The red-headed girl named Becky fumbled the return.

"Point—Red," Coach Daniels said. The red-jersied girls jumped up and down and high-fived each other, confident of another easy win.

The Blue team's morale plummeted, most of the girls already resigning themselves to another humiliating loss.

"Gee, one—nothing," Tiffany smiled from her side of the net. "Wah-wah-wah," she added—a mock-baby cry for Meilin's benefit.

Meilin turned to Jessie. "Switch places with Becky and set me up," she whispered. Jessie gave Meilin a questioning look. Meilin winked. Jessie smiled and nodded.

She went to the back row. "Trade with me," she said. Becky shrugged and traded spots with Jessie.

Red served again. The ball was long to the backcourt, but this time Jessie was there. She bumped-passed it high to the front row. Meilin leapt upward for the kill. Tiffany also jumped for what she figured was going to be an easy block.

But she was wrong. Meilin killed the ball with amazing strength and it rocketed past Tiffany to Red's mid-court. The ball hit the floor hard without contest.

"Blue!" Coach Daniels called.

The Blue team cheered, their spirits suddenly rising.

Jessie's eyes lit up at her friend's sudden voracity. "Oh, yeah!" she said to herself.

Meilin looked at Tiffany through the net. "Wah-wah-wah," she said, mocking Tiffany's earlier taunt.

Tiffany grit her teeth.

"Blue serves," Coach Daniels said, surprised herself with Meilin's play.

Jessie tossed the ball back to Becky and came forward, retaking her place next to Meilin. She looked at her friend.

Meilin winked again. Jessie smiled.

Becky served the ball. It was returned from Red's mid-court. Jessie moved into position for the intercept. "Set!" she called, and set the ball to the front line for Meilin.

Again, Meilin leapt up and spiked the ball, this time to the far corner of the red team's back line.

The volleyball traveled so fast, that again, the red team had no chance to react.

"Point—Blue!" Coach Daniels cried, now taking interest in what was happening on the court.

And so it was, over and over. Meilin took every set-up Jessie fed her and spiked the ball hard at the red team. The poor girls had no chance. Nor did Tiffany. Meilin even spiked the ball several times at her just to make the point that she was no longer the team's star. Within ten minutes, it was over, 21—1, a complete massacre.

"Game—Blue!" Coach Daniels shouted, then blew her whistle.

The blue team jumped with joy. They couldn't believe what happened. Nor could Tiffany. Her face was beet-red with anger. Meilin out-jumped her on every play. Tiffany had a tantrum on the court, blaming everyone on her team for the upset.

"Looks like I need to adjust the line-up," Coach Daniels said, looking at her clip-board. "Meilin, you wanna play first-string?"

"What!" Tiffany protested. "Miss Daniels..."

Coach Daniels ignored her. "Well?" she directed to Meilin. "We can use a good middle hitter!"

"But that's my slot!" Tiffany complained.

Coach Daniels waited for Meilin's reply.

"I'll play," Meilin said. "But only if the rest of the girls play too," she added, indicating her blue-jersied teammates.

Coach Daniels smiled. "Deal," she said. "Everybody plays. Standard rotation." The blue-jersied team jumped for joy.

"Locker room, girls," Coach Daniels said. "First game—Temple City, Wednesday!"

The girls followed the coach off the court.

Tiffany and Meilin remained behind.

"I don't know what your game is, Cheng," Tiffany growled. "But you better stay out of my way. The next four years belong to me!"

"No game," Meilin replied coolly, balancing a spinning volleyball on the tip of her finger. "And as far as the next four years go—they belong to everyone."

Tiffany glared at Meilin. "It's on, girl. It's *so* on..."

Meilin smiled. "Bring it," was all she said. Meilin turned and walked toward the locker room, leaving Tiffany standing in the center of the empty gymnasium.

Just before Meilin stepped off the court, her heightened monkey senses heard Tiffany utter, *"Chopstick!"*

Meilin shook her head with regret. She tossed the volleyball up in the air, did a back-flip and kicked it straight at Tiffany, without even looking.

The volleyball screamed across the court and hit Tiffany square in her face, breaking her perfect nose.

"My nose!" she screamed, holding her hands to her face to stem the flow of blood. "You broke my nose!"

At least that's what Meilin wanted to do.

She didn't, of course. That wasn't her Tao.

Meilin simply turned and held her hand up to her head, making the 'L' sign.

"Lose-ah!" Meilin mouthed with a smile. She then turned her back and walked away, laughing softly, "Eh-heh-heh," in her own monkey way.

Glossary

Bian-Lian *(biàn liǎn)* The performance art of changing vividly colored masks in fractions of a second.

Guanyin *(guan-yin)* The Taoist Goddess of Mercy.

Huli-jing *(húli jīng)* A Chinese fairy fox-spirit trickster, usually female, that can be good or bad.

Lijuan *(lee-jewan)* Beautiful and graceful.

Mao & Gou *(māo gǒu)* An expression "every *Mao* cat + *Gou* dog" used to say "anyone & everyone."

Meilin *(may-lin)* Beautiful jade or plum jade.

Sha Wujing *(shā wùjìng)* also **Sha Seng** aka Sandy Sand Monk. [*Sha* sand + *Wu* awareness + *Jing* purity, or *Sha* sand + *Seng* monk.]

Sun Wukong *(swun wùkōng)* The Monkey King [*Sun* monkey + *Wu* awareness + *Kong* vacuity, *Wukong* awakened to emptiness.]

Tao *(dao)* An Asian philosophical and religious belief that emphasizes balance and harmony with the natural order of the universe. It stresses humility, compassion and moderation. [The Way or Path.]

Xiang Yao *(shi-ang yao)* A serpent demon/sorcerer.

Yanluo *(yen-luo)* God of Death, in charge of the many levels of the Buddhist concept of hell.

Zhu Bajie *(zhū bājiè)* aka Pigsy the Pig Immortal made pig-demon for breaking the prohibitions of Buddhism. [*Zhu* pig + *Ba* eight + *Jie* prohibitions.]

To read more books in the series and follow

THE MANY ADVENTURES OF MEILIN

THE MONKEY KING'S DAUGHTER

visit your favorite bookstore
or log on to:

themonkeykingsdaughter.com